For my parents,
Dana Floyd Jennings and
Florence May Jennings

Live Free or Die

— Legend on
New Hampshire's
license plates

August 1975

Prologue

I SAT with my hands flat on the kitchen table. Sweat seeped from my forehead, rolled down my face, and dripped off my chin, making a wet spot at the neck of my T-shirt. Eyes shut, I cocked my head to one side like the table was whispering to me — Earl Duston.

I sopped up the shack's late-night sounds: The frigerator, working some too hard in the mugginess, shuddered; Ma's bed screeked as she was mauled by the heat; the faucet dripped; a cricket pined Hank Williams lonesome. Those sounds, family to me, made me feel a little better, settled my gut the way a baked potato slathered with butter did. But I missed Frank — miserable sonuvabitch that he was — snoring, snorting, and grunting out to the back porch. That longing put an edge on my black-assed mood, a mood that had a lot more to do with goddamned Denny Gamble than it did with Frank Sargent.

I shivered when I heard the mosquito. I'd been laying for it. I stopped brooding on Denny, doubled and undoubled my fists. The mosquito's ragged buzz, like a biplane over to the county fair, got louder. I opened my eyes, saw it flicker near the empty quarts of 'Gansett beer that lined the sink. It faded into shadow, came back, headed for the 40-watt bulb that shined dull from the ceiling. It circled the light slow and lazy, dipped, flew over my head, and settled on the plastic doily — scarred by cigarette burns — that Ma'd set on the table just so.

"Come on," I said. "Come on."

Buzzing louder, the mosquito lit out from the doily and flew slantways towards me. Skittering ear to chin, it brushed my cheek, raised an itch. Then and there I wanted to flatten it between my face and hand with a quick slap. But I had to wait for it to land, wait for it to steal my blood. That was the way the game had to be played. Denny'd said so; and he'd taught me. That was the tough part, the staying still, reeling it in. Once it landed and started to drink, you had it dicked. I flexed, felt my muscles knot, saw my blue veins bulge. The mosquito glided onto my arm — a hard-assed grin broke on my face — and swelled red.

When me and Denny were kids we'd tramp into the puckerbrush beyond the shack — towards the dark woods of Cedar Swamp — slouch against a tree, smoke the Luckies Denny'd clipped off his old man, and bushwhack mosquitoes. We must've killed thousands those summers. But I never got sick of watching mosquito bellies bloom red and perfect with our blood. We'd be ripe with bites, red blotches on our arms, chests, ankles, and faces — medals that we swore never to scratch. Only pussies itched mosquito bites.

But Denny played the devil with it, wrecked our mosquito game:

We're thirteen or so, smoking, shooting the shit, playing the game. A mosquito lights on Denny's hand. At first, he lets it be, studies it with his fisher-cat eyes. But then he plucks the mosquito off his hand, holds it by a wing — the mosquito doing a maniac's dance between his thumb and forefinger. He pulls on his Lucky, the tip glowing orange, and brings the cigarette to the mosquito, holds it just shy.

"Hey!" I say as the mosquito withers, dies.

I stare at Denny, but he doesn't look away, doesn't let on that he's done anything wrong. "Fuck you looking at?" he says.

"Nothing," I say.

That's all we ever said about it. We never played the mosquito game again. Well, almost never.

The mosquito stood cow-calm on my arm, siphoning blood. I raised my right arm, made a fist, cocked it, and held it over the mosquito, careful not to cast a shadow. My arm knotted tighter, sweat stung my eyes, my breath came harsh; I saw Denny looking at me, arms folded, smirking.

I hammered my left arm, which swelled red. The mosquito carcass — a black smudge — lay in a circle of blood the size of a penny. I scraped the mosquito off, dropped it onto the pile of dead on the table. I eyed those fifteen mosquitoes and thought of death given with pleasure and with no choice. Thought of Denny. Still saw him smirk, the knife in his hand, the Bible-black blood.

A mosquito bit my arm.

"You sonuvabitch!"

I punched, missed the mosquito. I hit my arm again. Again. Again — a retard trying to hurt himself. I slipped with a punch, and smacked the edge of the table.

"Fuck!"

Kneading my hand, I bent over, elbows on knees. Tears smoldered behind my eyes, but I wouldn't let them come.

"Goddamn," I said, shaking my head.

I closed my eyes, tried to gather in the shack's night

sounds, but all I could see, hear, and smell was Denny: Denny jamming the stick shift of his 'vette; Denny with his I-don't-give-a-shit grin skating on the black ice of Granite Lake; me and Denny clapping erasers in grammar school, ending up in an eraser fight.

I sat up, bit at my lower lip, stared at the dead mosquitoes. Drummed my feet. Sighed. Scratched my arm. Sighed again. Jumped up, slammed the chair against the wall, headed outdoors. I let the screen door *whang* shut behind me; that was usually a sweet sound, but I paid it no mind.

I stormed across the dooryard, but Ma's cedar-post clothesline stood in my way. I hit one of its thick posts with the heel of my hand, hit it again. I doubled my fist one finger at a time, slugged the post: knuckles crunched and my ears rang. I gritted my teeth, winced, and came with a roundhouse left. Post didn't duck. A couple fingers crumpled backwards. My ears and face burned, and the water round my eyes turned to real tears. I moved in on that post — a boxer who has the other guy limp on the ropes — and I banged at it and bashed at it, past the bark to the gray wood underneath, the white-hot pain a cure for what Denny'd done to me and what I'd done to Denny.

I truly believed I wanted to bust my hands.

Breath coming more slow and even, I looked at my hands in the moonlight: they were all skun up, bleeding, humming with the warmth of pain. I couldn't close them, and they hung heavy from my wrists — a couple of fingers splayed like a dead mosquito's legs, others bent, swollen. I peeled white skin off my knuckles with my teeth, the skin salty rubber. I slumped against the sagging clothesline. My work clothes hung on it, and even though they were fresh washed, they still reeked of the factory.

I looked to the shack, which was backlit by a full, orange moon. The shack reminded me of a wooden milk crate left outdoors too many winters — faded, cracked, warped. I did have the woods beyond the shack, but I wasn't even sure of that no more. Even in the moonlight those woods — the Granite edge of Cedar Swamp — held their darkness.

Most Graniters steered clear of Cedar Swamp. Mosquito-ridden, they said. Bogs there that could suck a man down like an undertow. Snakes thick as telephone poles slithered there, snapping turtles that could rip off a leg. Bear and wildcat still roamed the swamp, which stretched for miles between Granite and New Falls. A few old-timers still ventured in to hunt deer, bear, and the cats, or to gather the berries, grapes, and rhubarb that grew wild. But for the most part, I was the only person I knew of who slogged through the swamp regular — except for Azalea Kelley. But she lived there.

In half an hour's hike I could be away from everything and everybody; in an hour I could be in the heart of the swamp. But I hadn't gone since the night me and Denny spent there. I'd spoiled it by taking him. The swamp'd been mine. But I'd brought Denny there. That had made the difference.

I fell asleep against the cedar post, hands cradled in my lap.

June–July 1975

1

I'D FOUGHT for sleep all night, tossing and turning, grappling with heat and bad dreams. I woke up more beat than when I went to bed. My eyes burned, my crotch and armpits were slick with sweat. Like most work mornings, pains jabbed my gut. Only Tuesday, but I wished to hell it was Friday.

It was one of those hot Junes that catches most everyone by surprise after a cool, wet New Hampshire spring. Only six in the morning, and already the sun — a dark red wound rising in the east — dripped heat on Granite. Heavy-handed heat that strangled the morning breeze and ripped out the songbirds' throats.

Shack sat quiet. Ma and Frank never woke before I did; usually, they were sleeping off the night before. Sitting up, I wobbled between sleep and work. Finally, I took a deep breath, kicked off my sweaty sheet, and swung my legs over the side of the bed. Feet on the floor, I hunched over, held my gut; pains got worse every morning. It felt like I was trying to digest razor blades. Just thinking about the factory made it hurt worse. It was okay once I got to work. But at the start of another day, my gut would mutiny. Heat the way it was, I knew I'd be taking some days off — factory be fucked. Crusty, my cat, scratched at the back door. So I pushed myself out of bed, pulled on some undershorts, and walked down to the kitchen, stairs groaning as I went.

The big tomcat looked the way I felt: left eye closed and swollen purple, blood caked around his nose and ears, yellow fur ripped from his coat. He rubbed against my legs, looked up at me, and croaked a rusty-hinged purr.

"What a mess," I said. He purred again.

I got a wet cloth and washed his battered face. You'd think a big goon of a cat like him could take care of himself. But he was always getting his ass beat. Good mouser, though; left shredded mice on the back steps. Sometimes there'd be a bird or a chipmunk — Ma didn't like that. But what the hell, a cat's a cat. Right?

The turtle lay splattered in the road like a pumpkin at Hallowe'en. A fresh death; its orange guts oozed out as the first flies showed. A middling turtle, no bigger than a pie plate, with flecks of red, orange, and yellow painted on its shriveled idiot head. I stopped, wanted to do something. But a turtle squashed in the road? I kept moving.

Woods lined Meeks Road, and in the early morning not much sun sifted through the leaf cover. But it was hot anyways, and I broke out in a sweat as I loped up the road. It wasn't that I was in any hurry to get to work; that's just the way I walk. Couldn't slow down. I'd walk like that to the store, in Cedar Swamp — probably to my own hanging.

I come from a family of great walkers. Bub, my real old man, used to say that the first time Grandma Jenny left Grandpa Ora, she walked out on him in the middle of one of their raise-the-dead rhubarbs and hoofed it from New

Falls all the way to Alton Bay, some fifty miles away. When I was a kid Ma used to take me on long walks in the woods, especially when we lived on the farm in Hampstead. But that was a long time ago. And when Bub was young he used to run in the footraces they held over to Manchester. But that was before I was born, before he took to drinking so.

Meeks Road opened out about opposite Granite Barrel — a filthy, concrete rectangle that squatted in the old Britton sandpit. Black stacks jutted from the roof, already puking steam, dust, and smoke into the air; thousands of 55-gallon steel drums stretched from the back of the factory into the pit for a good half mile. Granite Barrel cleaned steel drums for industry, and most of those drums held the leavings of all kinds of bad shit: poisons, resins, acids, oils. You name it; if it could kill you, we probably cleaned it. I looked both ways, crossed Route 49, and walked down the gravel driveway to the factory.

An orange General Electric drum lay half buried in the sand, rust-jagged. Oil seeped from a Mobil drum flipped on its side. A Lilly Chemical drum, the color of a candy apple and sporting a skull-and-crossbones sticker, leaned against the factory, bent double. Other drums stood in wobbly stacks; the bottom drums, gutted by rust, were leaky, crumbling, and bee-ridden. Ruts like craters and puddles wide as swimming holes pocked the yard. But the water in those puddles hadn't fallen from the sky — hadn't rained all month. It had leached from the factory. Near the road, three willow saplings drooped like young girls brushing their hair. Backed up to the loading platforms, new trailer trucks sat pretty, the sun glinting off the chrome Mack bulldogs on the tractors' hoods, the words GRANITE BARREL stenciled in bold letters on the trailers. The tractors, bright blue, red, or yellow, had names: Julie, Bev, Valerie.

But the first thing that hit you at the factory was the smell. It wasn't a smell you could reason with. Some days you could sniff it more'n a mile away: fumes from a bad-assed brew of acids, paints, oils, solvents, black dust, stagnant water, steam, piss, puke, sweat, exhaust, and chemicals whose names I couldn't begin to pronounce. A smell come to stay. It clung to the brick, the machines, the steel drums, the joints in Marcel's breast pocket. It lingered, hung on our bodies and clothes, dogged us home. We scrubbed our skin red and raw to get it off, but we could never get the smell out of our clothes. On a Monday morning it could curdle your stomach and make you turn around and walk back home. If the factory'd up and vanished one night, there still would've been the smell, permanent as a gravestone.

Then there were the guys I worked with. Homer sat in his black '63 Ford Falcon — that car was cherry — downing a can of Bud. Marcel and Braley crouched in the bed of Marcel's beat-up pickup and did a joint, Braley giggling. Dirty Willy slinked in the factory's shadows, bent over, lips working: a rat. And G.I. Joe, ballicky bare-assed except for a jock, stood on the roof of his '67 Dodge Dart and did calisthenics: jumping jacks, toe touchers, situps, pushups — all the while the Dart's roof going *whump, whump, whump*. When it rained, water pooled in the dent on the roof. G.I. said he did the exercises to keep away the demons that followed him around the factory. And that, too, is why he had a swastika tattooed on his dick. No shit. He showed it to us once.

No one looked up when I walked into the lunchroom: Murphy, hunched over one of the baby-shit green Formica tables, studied a week-old *Manchester Union Leader* (the *Onion Liar*, we called it); Lurch patched a hole in his rubber boots; Dirty Willy, who'd scuttled in from outdoors, picked his nose; Andy, Double Murphy, and Barnaby talked about the Red Sox game — Sox'd blown a three-run lead in the ninth and lost in eleven; Ray and Bill drank ice tea out of Ray's Thermos; everyone else just sat there out of focus, staring at the scummy cement floor, waiting for the buzzer. Rusty and Dog weren't in yet — they were usually late anyways — and Dickie had a week's vacation. I picked my way towards the time clock, a couple of guys grunting, "Mornin', Earl." I plucked my card out of the rack (they'd spelled my name wrong again — Dustin this time) and slid it into the clock — *chunk, chunk.*

The lunchroom had been an afterthought, a cement square slapped against the rest of the shop. They'd put in three bench tables, a tonic machine, and a water cooler, and called it a lunchroom. Too small to fit everyone; a lot of the guys either sat outside or stood by their machines inside the factory to wait for work to start. I never walked into that hole any sooner'n I had to. I squeezed in next to Bill and Ray.

"Heard it's going to be another hot one, Earl," Bill said. "Heard it on the weather this morning."

"Feels it," I said.

"S'posed to go up into the nineties after noon. Going to be a hot one."

"Sucks."

"Yup. Everything sucks round here."

"Fuckin' right," said Ray, who never said much except fuckin' right. "Fuckin' right."

"Least you got a vacation coming pretty quick," I said to Bill. "Right?"

"Yup," Bill said. "End of next week. And I'm just going to stay home for two weeks and screw the old lady all day long."

"Fuckin' right," Ray said.

Bill and Ray laughed. I nodded.

"What's a matter there, Billy?" asked Murph, who was sitting across from us. "Ain't you getting enough?"

Bill was about to answer him, but the clock clicked to seven and the buzzer blatted, killing the laughing and talking quick, the way a cop does when he rounds a corner where a bunch of kids are raising hell. Murph left his newspaper on the table; Lurch, his boots fixed, pulled them on; Dirty Willy smeared a snot on the window, stood up, and sniffed his armpits; Andy, Double Murphy, and Barnaby forgot about the Red Sox and glared up the stairs into the factory; Ray and Bill chugged the last of their tea; and everyone scowled at the time clock as they trudged up the steps into the factory for another day of work.

I stood at a doorway about five foot high and four foot wide. A steel track stretched from the doorway outdoors to the burner: a big-as-a-barn furnace that burned cleaned the guts of 55-gallon steel drums. The track carried the drums through the burner, then to me.

My T-shirt leeched to me. Sweat streaked my face. My eyes smarted, and my hands, inside rubber gloves, were being boiled in their own juices. A drum bumped through the doorway, parts of it still glowing orange. I grabbed it — face and arms soaking up its heat — and in one motion jerked it up and stacked it three high on the row of drums to my right, banging it against the others. About fifteen seconds later another drum thumped through, and I did it again. Another drum, same thing. Every five drums or so I plunged my hands into the water bucket I kept near the door. The water cooled my hands some, made my blisters feel good. Usually, I didn't have to stack so many drums. As they banged through, I just shoved them down to Andy, who ran the blaster. But Johnson, the fucking foreman, had us pushing so many drums through to fill some big order that Andy couldn't keep up. And if Andy, who's the hardest worker I've ever seen, couldn't keep up, then Johnson was pushing too hard. I usually handled some fifteen hundred drums a day, or one about every twenty seconds. But they were ramming them through the burner every ten, fifteen seconds. That meant they weren't getting burned good. Meant more ashes and cinders singed my face, neck, and arms — pissing me off no end. Meant Andy had to blast each drum that much longer to grind it down to bare steel.

Hadn't had a drum in a minute or so, so I poked my head out the doorway and saw that the guys at the burner were unloading a truck. I slumped down on the crate next to my bucket, pressed my back against the grimy wall, pulled off my gloves — scarred and thinning — and plopped them in the water.

The factory was lit by blinking, crackling overhead lights and muted shafts of sun that trickled through dust-covered windows. That light reflected dull on the hundreds of fresh-painted drums stacked three high and the murky pools of water ripe with chemical sludge and caustic acid. Wires and cables trailed from the ceiling — creepers in a machine jungle. Worst of all was the black steel-shot dust, which hung in the air like cancer come to life.

That steel dust billowed from Andy's machine, the blaster, which roared and groaned as it bombarded each drum with thousands of pieces of steel shot that stripped it to bare bones. Working in front of a revolving steel door, Andy fed two drums into the blaster and took another two out, shoving the clean drums to Ray at the roller. Andy was smudged with steel dust. It clung to his hair and clothes, got under his fingernails, matted the hair on his arms. Pieces of steel shot worked their way into his ears, nose, mouth, and the corners of his goggled eyes as sweat gushed down his dust-black face. He told me that every night after work his wife touched his eyes, ears, and nose with a magnet to gather the steel shot that didn't come out when he washed up.

A drum thudded through the doorway. I sighed, stood up, snagged it, and slammed it onto the stack. Andy slid drums in and out the blaster slick as shit. Ray shoved drums on and off the roller, flattening dents. Barnaby pulled down a drum, cocked it at a 45-degree angle, snapped his wrist, and sent it spinning, tilted like a car balanced on two wheels; Marcel, barely touching it, kept it going on its way to Rusty loading a truck — center-short-to-home, drum after drum rumbling on the cement floor. Porky, down to the other end, could send three drums spinning at once: one with each hand and one with his over-the-belt gut.

The machines boomed, banged, and belched, giving the ragged bass beat to our work. After a while you stopped hearing the noise and moved to your own rhythm, your body reacting to the drums, your mind escaping the factory, thinking about Swett's Pond on a Friday night, a cold Bud, getting laid. Anything but the goddamned factory.

Don't know why I kept remembering this, but sometimes when we were really humping, when it seemed the work'd never end, I'd get wrapped up in this memory of when I wasn't any more'n four years old:

I'm sitting under the kitchen table — all hemmed in by the chair legs and table legs — not even playing with anything, but sitting there real quiet. The morning sun hits my face, warms me. And I see the dust specks dancing in the sunlight.

That was it. But I kept thinking about it — the stillness,

the quiet, the sun. That kind of daydreaming got fingers slashed, faces burned, ribs broke. But you couldn't get around it. You couldn't think about the factory, about work all the time, or you'd go crazy. Maybe crazy as Dirty Willy.

Andy shut the blaster; its dying whine made me look up. He shoveled fresh steel shot into the blaster's dark mouth, his arm muscles swelling as he heaved the steel in. Finished feeding the blaster, he motioned me to stop the track from the burner — jabbing his stubby finger in the air. Andy sucked on a Pall Mall as I walked over, his eyes ringed by white circles where he'd worn his goggles.

"Hell of a day, huh?" I said.

"Real pisser," he said. "I'd like to take a shovel full of this shot and stick it up Johnson's ass."

"He's been on the rag for two weeks."

"Tell me something I don't know."

Andy took one last, long pull on his cigarette, dropped it, heeled it out. Then he coughed hard, hawked up a gob of blood and phlegm, and spit it on the floor, where it rolled a couple inches in the black dust.

"Got to go down the blaster, shovel out some shot," he said. "Won't start up for another fifteen, twenty minutes."

"Don't rush," I said.

"I won't."

He pulled on his goggles and walked behind the blaster, scuffling through the steel shot heaped on the floor. He grabbed a ladder leaning against the wall and slid it into the gap between the blaster and the floor — a gap just big enough for a man to fit — dropped in a shovel and two five-gallon pails. He crept down the ladder into the blaster's black gut.

When Andy'd been out sick with some lung thing the winter before, I'd helped Barnaby shovel out the pit, which was about eight foot wide and eight foot deep. On a good blaster, the pit only had to be cleaned every month or so. But our blaster was in such shitty shape that it hurled as much shot into the pit as it did at the drums. It had to be shoveled at least once a day, sometimes twice.

Down there it's dark and reeks of steel dust, tinged by the sweet smell of grease. Me and Barnaby worked back to back, shoveling shot into pails, with me always willing to carry the heavy loads up the ladder to get out of the pit. Even though there's two foot of clearance, I felt cramped, closed in. I got the feeling I used to get when I squeezed under the bed to hide from Bub when he was rip-shit. That's a hell of a feeling. Seven years old and knowing your old man wants to beat the fuck out of you. Ducking into your room, hoping he doesn't know, wriggling under the bed, and sucking in the dust and dirt, trying not to sneeze or cough, head pounding, hands sweating. And it's dark. So dark. But his fists, those heavy hooks, are a lot worse than hiding under the bed; his hard hands always pay off — you aren't tougher than they are. At least under the bed you can close your eyes, double your fists, grit your teeth, and hold out. It's worst under the bed when you hear his footsteps in the room. The work boots thumping on the wood floor, slow, halting, searching, then softer, fading.

Blaster didn't faze Andy, though. When he wanted a butt break and didn't want to hassle with Johnson, he climbed down into the pit, pulled up a pile of steel shot, and fired up a smoke.

Andy dug into the shot — *scrunch, scrunch* — as I headed back to my crate.

"F-f-fuckin' J-Johnson," Dirty Willy said as I walked by. "B-bastard."

Dirty Willy pulled blasted drum covers from his machine and put dirty ones in their place, a thundercloud of dust hanging over him. We called him Dirty Willy because when he came to work he wasn't any cleaner than when he'd left the night before. You couldn't tell what was dirt and what was skin on his stubbled face and bald head. What hair he had shot back from his temples and looked more like feathers than hair. With his squinty eyes and stupid but solemn face, he looked like a brain-damaged owl.

He owned land over to New Falls, raised chickens on it and sold eggs. He also bought scrap metal and other junk to sell to salvage yards. He lived in a trailer-truck box the company gave him after one of the drivers plowed it into a bridge. About fifty foot off the road the box sat up on blocks, GRANITE BARREL painted on its side in big purple letters. And almost always, Willy'd be sitting on top the box, cradling a chicken, waving to people as they went by, looking like some demented weather vane — crazy north, south, east, and west.

Goddamned Willy. It was him got me my job. He's the one told Frank and Ma he could get me in, and they made me quit school and go to work. I should've run off. But I figured Ma needed me around to save her from Frank. Talk about dumb.

They'd talked about me quitting school before, Frank and Ma had, but I never paid it no mind. This time it all started one night at supper about a month before they made me quit.

"Willy tells me he can get you in at the barrel factory," Frank says, sopping up bean juice with brown bread.

"Ain't interested," I says.

"It'd sure help us out," Ma says. "Frank don't make much working for the town."

"Let him work there, then," I say.

"You know I can't do work like that," Frank says. "Causes too much pressure in my head. Take it in a minute if I could."

"Right," I say.

"I would," he says.

"Booze causes a lot of pressure in your head, too," I say. "Don't see you stop drinking."

"You watch your mouth," he says, "or I'll shut it up for you real fast."

I dip my spoon into the beans.

"It'd be real steady," Ma says. "Willy says the pay's good. Sure could use the money."

"School's steady, too," I say.

"Sure could use the money," Ma says again. "Bub ain't been sending no divorce money."

That's the way it went that last month. Then, the week before Thanksgiving, Frank tells me I have to move out if I don't quit school and go to work. Ma doesn't say a thing.

I started at the factory the Monday after Thanksgiving.

"Fuck's the story?"

Johnson.

He walked towards the blaster, saw Andy wasn't there, scowled, headed at me.

"Where's Andy?" he snarled. "We ain't on vacation."

"He . . ." I started. But Johnson wheeled away towards the blaster. Dirty Willy grinned at me, flashing his yellow stumps.

Johnson paced in front of the blaster like he had a hornet shoved up his ass. He was one of those guys who'd been with the company so long that Old Man Fecteau had had to either fire him or make him foreman. He had a pinched, weasel face, the kind of guy who'd lick shit off your boots if you paid him enough. Not only that, he'd say he liked it. It wouldn't've been so bad if he knew how to do his job. But he didn't know his ass from his elbow. Didn't know how to treat a man like a man. All he knew was push, push, push.

Andy knew more about Johnson's job than Johnson did, and it burned Andy something fierce to take shit from him. We all figured Andy should've been made foreman when Big Tuck'd quit the year before. But Johnson was Fecteau's pet. Andy wasn't nobody's pet.

Johnson glanced at his watch, looked up, glared at me. "Get the fuck to work," he shouted, his neck getting red. "Help Willy there stack his covers." I flipped him the bird.

He turned his back on me and stared at the blaster, looking like he thought he could make Andy appear if he stared hard enough. He shrugged, grabbed a drum, and pushed the blaster's green start button. The blaster groaned to life, spewing steel-shot dust.

I was on him in a second, knocked him away, and jammed the red off button.

"You fucking idiot! Andy's in there!"

Johnson staggered back, face white, eyes wide and blinking. Dust puked from the pit in heavy, rolling clouds.

"Andy!" I yelled. "You all right?!"

No answer.

"Andy!"

Then a steady *clomp-clomp-clomp* up the ladder. A gloved hand poked through the dust. Then Andy's hard, black face.

"Who?"

"Johnson."

He coughed a cough that jerked his body so hard it looked shot full of lightning — a deathbed cough. He leaned against the blaster. When the coughing stopped, he straightened up. That's when I saw the small points of red oozing from his face, the blood discolored in the caked dust. Looked like someone'd taken a needle, jabbed a few hundred times.

"Andy?"

He stepped around me, and walked around the corner of the blaster; Johnson stood next to the roller. One by one, the sounds of work stopped: no drums clanged; no steel shot rattled; no paint guns whoosh-whooshed; no hammers pounded. Nothing. Just the hum of electricity, the hiss of compressed air.

They'd come to watch — Murphy and Double Murphy, G.I. Joe, Rusty, Ray, Dirty Willy, Lurch, Marcel, Braley, everyone — silent, arms folded. Johnson sweated like the pig he was, gross drops beading on his forehead and upper lip. He glanced around — too quick, too skittish — hemmed in by the drums, us. The only way out was through Andy, whose shoulders drooped as he trudged towards Johnson.

"Andy," Johnson said. "I . . ."

Andy's gloves dropped from his hands. He stopped about four foot short of Johnson, who was backed against the roller. Andy tugged off his goggles, let them fall, too. Johnson squirmed. Andy just stared at him — Johnson looking down and sideways — blood and dust painting his face. It seemed they stood that way a full minute, and we stood as still and silent as they did. The trout was hooked; we wanted to see him landed. When Johnson saw that the blood from Andy's face was beginning to drip on the floor, he tried to run. But we held fast, delivered him up to Andy.

A left doubled Johnson over.

Another left busted his nose; blood gushed.

A right knocked him on his back.

Johnson looked up at Andy, flinched. But Andy paid him no mind. He walked on and over Johnson: stepped on his balls, his gut, his chest, down the aisle, and out the door. Johnson whimpered. The rest of us stood in churchy silence.

◢ 2

FRANK SARGENT hid on his porch, guzzling Black Label beers the way his shitbox Chevy swilled gasoline. He'd been sitting there since nine that morning, knocked on his ass by the heat. Air was as thick and still as dirty motor oil; no leaves rustled, no dogs barked, no cars shuddered by on Meeks Road. All he could hear was that whine — peculiar to hot days — which pierces your inner ear, then stops short quick as it started.

Slumped bare-chested in his cellar-smelling overstuffed chair, Frank stared through the porch screen to the woods beyond the back step. Through those woods lay Cedar Swamp and, farther on, the Boston & Maine Railroad. On those mornings when he woke up and could hear the wail of the B & M rise low and mournful over the swamp, he knew, without looking out the window, that it was raining or about to. On those gray mornings, Frank (who'd done his time in North Country logging camps) longed to be on that freight as it rumbled through the woods to Maine and Canada. Though it was a blistering afternoon, the train howled in his head as he drank and stared into the woods. He wanted to fade into the trees, slog through the swamp, and hitch a ride on the freight as it left New Hampshire behind.

"Fuck it," he said, cracking another Black Label. "Just fuck it."

After one pull, he tried to balance the half-empty bottle on the chair's arm, setting it down the way a young father'll stand up his first son and urge him to walk. The bottle wobbled between his thumb and forefinger — first listing thumbwards, then tilting fingerwards. He kept at it, jaw set and forehead knotted, tried to find that sweet spot between chair arm and beer bottle that'd flip gravity the bird. He had the look of a kid trying to bait a fishing hook with a sausage-thick nightcrawler that needs to be bent four times before it's snug. But finally the bottle spun from his hands — even as he grabbed for it — and fell, splashing beer all over his dungarees.

"Shit!"

He plucked the near-empty bottle from his lap, sucked down the last suds. Without looking, he tossed the bottle to the left, towards his beer barrel — a 55-gallon steel drum heaped with empties — in the porch's far corner. The bottle smacked the drum and shattered, showering the porch in specks and splinters of brown beer glass.

"Damn."

Norma called from inside, "Frank? You all right?"

"Why don't you shut the fuck up and mind your own business?" he snapped back.

No answer.

"Nosy cunt."

He belched, long and loud, glorying in it, then considered his wet lap with a kind of sadness, his brown eyes heavy lidded. He ran an index finger over the wetness, licked it — a faint beer taste mixed with finger salt. He sighed, looked towards the woods again as if he expected something, someone.

Frank had a drinker's face, bloodshot eyes and caved-in cheeks that sharpened his cheekbones. Wasn't a handsome face, anyways — stubbled, bushy black eyebrows, scars like chickens' feet at the corners of his eyes — and it looked the worse for the drinking. But he didn't have the nose. He was proud of that. Didn't have the gross, overripe tomato of a nose like Carl or Elmer. One of those alky noses, with the red veins fit to bust and pores big enough to hold a pencil. Didn't have it. Could still do a day's work, too — when he felt like it. He wasn't as strong as when he'd worked the logging camps, but he hadn't gone to seed, either. He could still split a cord of wood. His fists could still make the thunder roll.

Trying to stand, he fell back twice, raising a small dust cloud each time he hit the chair. He waited a few seconds, tried to get up again. Couldn't.

Slouched in the chair, he ran his hand over his head, nibbled on his lower lip, scratched his sandpaper chin. Sweat coming harder now, he flexed and unflexed his fingers, gulped air. Then, grabbing both arms of the chair, he lurched forward and up. The backs of his legs strained against the chair as he seesawed at the brink of standing. But his ass sagged and he fell, a man pulled back to bed by an unsatisfied lover.

"Screw this," he said, and he slithered off the chair, the coarse cushions strawberrying his back.

On all fours, he limped doglegged to the card table next to the beer barrel, rose to begging position, placed his hands flat on the table, and pushed himself up. Wobbly, he studied the table: Bicycle playing cards were strewn all over from last night's poker game, and a three-quarters-empty bottle of Pabst stood in front of Elmer's seat. Frank ignored the cards, snatched up Elmer's orphaned Pabst, and downed the piss-warm brew in one slug, wiping the dribble from his chin with his bare arm. He hadn't even eyeballed the bottle's innards to check for cigarette butts.

"What a life," he muttered, and looked to the woods again.

He staggered from the porch into the front room, where the heat was worse, hunkered down like an unwanted uncle set on staying for supper. Feeling like someone'd wrapped a wet wool blanket around his face, Frank leaned against the couch to catch his breath. Over the couch hung a handmade rug he'd bought Norma the time they drove up to Nova Scotia: a brown deer stands tall against a navy blue night sky, but the big buck looks vexed, sniffs the air. One of the buck's forelegs wasn't as brown as the rest of him, though; Frank'd leaned up against the wall one night and puked on him.

Frank stumbled into the kitchen, where Norma was making supper. Gaining the center of the small room, he announced, "I'm going to Buzzell's to get another six."

Norma didn't look up from the onions and peppers sizzling in her frying pan.

"Got any money?" he asked her. "All I need's couple bucks."

"All I got's food money," she said.

"Two bucks."

Holding the spatula tight, she stirred the vegetables faster.

"Just a couple bucks," he said.

She glanced at him, wiping her sweaty palms on her apron. He swayed, looking at her, his chest heaving.

A man, my man, standing drunk in the middle of my

kitchen, she thought. Why's it always been like this? My father, my brothers, Bub, Frank, all the others . . .

There'd been Reggie, who'd had fleas in his goatee, brayed better'n a donkey, and always cried when they made love — big scalding tears, like a little boy whose dog lays sprawled and splattered out to the highway.

She'd meant to marry Harry. A sliver of steel sheared off some machine at the junkyard — where he'd worked some twenty years — and burrowed into his skull. It'd taken him a month to die.

Eddie, a Filipino who was always saying, "Don't eat that. That no good, make you fart." She'd gotten rid of him because he'd laughed when Governor Wallace of Alabama'd been shot.

Albert died of the cancer up to the V.A. hospital in Manchester. Wasn't much of a man, though. Spent most of his time building helicopters, ships, and airplanes out of cardboard boxes and toilet paper tubes. All she could smell when they'd made love was airplane glue; all she could feel were his tacky hands on her breasts. She'd burned the models after he died.

And Joe. He beat Earl up something fierce once because Earl'd won him at a game of checkers. Earl'd only been ten.

She'd tell you that she loved Frank, had loved them all. That's what she'd say. But hers was a face carved by betrayal — given and received. She'd been pretty once: light brown hair, face as delicate as a teacup handle. But hard living and hard drinking had eroded the once-smooth skin, gouged out gorges and chasms. The light brown hair had curdled to early gray; her blue eyes were hard, glazed — marbles fried in a skillet. Norma's face was earned, and it trembled between anger and fear.

"Frank Sargent. You left this house yesterday morning with twenty g.d. dollars in your pocket," she said. "Where'd it go?"

"Fuck's the difference?"

"Don't you talk to me like that."

"Give me the money."

The argument cleared Frank's head the way a cold wind'll whip down from Canada and blow a storm out of the sky. He stepped closer, and her back stiffened. She turned to her cooking, stirred even faster, the spatula scraping the frying pan. Between the heat of the kitchen and the heat of her fear, she felt she might pass out. Sweat stitched her eyes and it got harder to concentrate on the onions and peppers. Smiling now, Frank walked to the stove.

She shuddered when he planted his hands on her hips and hissed in her ear, "Give me the money, cunt."

She knew what was coming. No getting around it. She hoped it wasn't so, but his face was set in that hurting way — a kid who's decided to shove a firecracker up a stray cat's ass — with that hateful smile. She knew that look the way she knew his body in the dark.

His breath, a mulch of tobacco, beer, and rotting food, almost made her gag. But she didn't look at him, kept stirring. He dug his fingers into her hips, pressed his body to hers, and started humping her the way a small dog'll hump a stranger's leg.

"Give it to me, Norma," he said, thrusting, banging her knees against the stove. "Give it to me."

"Stop it, Frank."

"Give it to me, Norma. Give it."

He sank his fingers into her arms. She couldn't move; the frying pan spit hot grease at her. The bitter sting of burning onions and peppers filled her nose, started the tears. Frank was still smiling when she dropped the spatula on the floor.

"Give it to me, Norma. Give it to me."

"Cut the shit, Frank."

He drove at her harder, harder, her knees drumming against the oven door; looked like she was fucking the stove. A tight grin lit Frank's face.

"Frank . . ."

"Give it to me, Norma! Give it!"

"You're hurting me, you sonuvabitch!"

All he wanted was to keep on hearing the B & M as it rumbled along the tracks of his head. Another six-pack'd do that. All he had to do was sit on the porch, down the beer, listen, and wait. He could've heard it right then, if only she'd shut up and let him. But her pissing and moaning made it hard to hear. He'd have to quiet her down.

He wrenched her around, a partner in a hateful square dance. She didn't struggle, knew it was hopeless. Once it started, the ritual always ran its course.

"My arm, Frank."

His first punch knocked her on the floor, split her lip. But all Norma could think about was the peppers and onions burning on the stove, the smoke filling the kitchen, smarting her eyes.

◢

First hot days of the year always made my ass drag something wicked, and I was just looking forward to a couple cold ones, washing up, supper, and the Red Sox on the radio.

Ma's scream burst from the shack, window-rattling loud, the shriek of a small, fierce animal — a fisher cat, say —

that's got itself caught in some trap and don't like it one goddamned bit. There weren't nothing helpless about that scream, though. Scared, but not helpless. I hauled ass towards the house, work boots spitting gravel. I knew what was going on — again. Been going on ever since I could remember. If it wasn't Frank, it was some other asshole. Never could understand why Ma took up with Frank after the way Bub'd whaled on her. You'd a thought she could've found some guy who had balls enough not to beat on a woman.

First time I ever saw Frank smack Ma I'd just come home from school. I walks in and see him crack her one in the face, knocking her into the kitchen table. I drop my books, take a run at him, fists up. But he picks me up and whungs me through the screen door. Way I crashed through that door and tumbled down those steps I thought he broke my neck. I was stiff for two weeks, and plucking slivers out my ass for another three.

But I'd filled out since then, which sure as hell kept Ma's buns pink and soft. When I was around, I always ended up taking the beating meant for her. Me and Ma might've had our differences — big differences — but you can't sit on your ass and let some bastard maul your mother and still stand when you take a leak.

When I saw smoke pouring out the back door I thought Frank'd gone ape-shit and set the house on fire. But once I got inside — sucking down that bitter dump-smelling smoke — I saw the food burned up on the stove.

Ma lay in the doorway between the living room and the kitchen: a stunned, hurt animal trying to drag herself out of harm's way — a woodchuck, say, nicked just so by a swerving car. Frank stood over her, doubling and undoubling his fists, his back to me; neither of 'em had heard me run in.

I jumped him — Frank Sargent didn't deserve no warning — monkey-hugging his back as the two of us staggered to the floor. Ma crawled into a corner and curled up the way one of those black and orange wooly-bear caterpillars will when you touch it. I shoved Frank off my chest; he wasn't with it yet, didn't know what'd happened; and pushing him was like pushing a dead Cadillac uphill. It might sound slow, but what happened next happened quick. It always takes longer to tell a fight than for the brawling to be done with.

Frank tried to stand, but I dove at his legs, knocking him down again. Pinning him, my knees buried in his ribs, I swung wild — the smoke watering my eyes — and clipped his nose hard enough to bleed it. Blood seeped into his mouth and he spit it in my face, where it scalded. Ticked off, I pasted his face three or four good ones, skinning my knuckles and uprooting a couple of his stumpy teeth.

"There!" I shouted, fielding his blood-flecked teeth and bouncing them off his ornery puss. "There! How's it taste?"

I'd never gotten that good a jump on him, never banged him so hard, and those wolf eyes of his narrowed. But instead of putting him away when I had the chance, I gloated, gloried in his surprise. It was like teasing a garter snake with a rake, goading it to hiss and strike before killing it.

When I saw Frank's eyes go granite I tried to crack him again. But he'd worked an arm free. He blocked my punch and elbowed my throat. When I hesitated, went a little too slack, he snapped his leg back and kneed me in the nuts, sending me ass-over-bandbox. I swear I thought someone'd stretched out my balls and hammered on 'em. My ears rang and my eyes watered; I gulped for air, but all I swallowed was that greasy, stinging, stinking smoke still spewing from the stove. Nursing the pain, hand still trying to convince my crotch that we weren't getting no trial separation, I twitched on the gritty linoleum.

Frank started kicking. Like some kind of goddamned second-grade girl, the pussy bastard kicked: my ribs, legs, gut, head. His heavy black work boots thudding away with the wallop of rotgut whiskey, he booted my ass all the way across the kitchen floor, out the back door, down the steps, and into the dooryard. It was all I could do to cover my head.

He let up — his leg likely getting tired — and I wobbled to my knees. My balls throbbed. My whole body ached. It felt like somebody'd run me through the blaster, couldn't tell whether it was blood or sweat oozing down my face. Frank looked down at me, his filthy grin stretched back to his ear hairs. I figured he might've cooled, that it might be over. I didn't want no more. But then there was that big, black boot bearing down on me. I couldn't duck, just turned my head and closed my eyes. The boot connected just so, right above the ear. My head snapped back, whole body shuddered; head rang with the banging and clanging of steel drums as I hit the ground. But I wasn't knocked out. Sure, the dooryard spun some too fast and I saw Frank through what looked to be a wall of fire, but I weren't out.

Grinning his stump-toothed grin, Frank bent over me, his whiskers scratching my face. The flat-beer smell of his breath made me want to puke. Something pleased with himself, he said, "Had enough, boy?"

I didn't say nothing.

"Had enough?"

If he'd just let me be, had just walked away, that would've been that. But he had to pick, keep yakking.

The hate built quick in me — a nasty summer storm.

And the more I thought about the beatings and the near beatings, the fiercer that storm brewed. I was sick of Frank's boots stomping on my face, sick of Ma squalling for help, sick and tired of every fist that'd ever nailed me for no better reason than that I was just a kid. I imagined that I saw Bub's face leering out of Frank's. I hadn't seen *that* prick since he walked out on us. I winced as I saw Bub's ham hands come a-crashing; God, he used to beat me. And that was the least of it. The things he did to me . . .

But there was the cool spring day when Bub brought me home a baseball glove. I must've been seven and I felt like the luckiest kid in town to have an old man who'd buy me a baseball glove: Tony Conigliaro model, with Tony C.'s autograph stamped in black on the thumb. My favorite ball player. I loved that glove, its leather smell, its leather taste. To some folks, baseball is the smell of fresh-cut grass or of beer and roasted peanuts. But to me, leather is the smell of baseball.

Finally, one blizzard morning, Bub lit out for good. We lived over to Hardscrabble Road then, and Bub says he's driving over to Roy's Acres to pick up some homemade doughnuts and a jug of cider. It's snowing like hell, and when Bub opens the back door the wind, like it's been laying for him, rips the door from his hands and bangs it wide. Snakes of snow slither across the threshold and, for a second, the storm swirls in the kitchen as wind-driven pinwheels of snow burst through the open door. Bub staggers back — "Fuck!" — grabs the door by the knob, and starts pulling it shut against the wind, straining at it like he's dragging some stubborn mutt tied to a hank of rope. Once he gets the door shut, he tugs his hat down over his ears and, head down, plods to the Chevy.

And never comes back. Me and Ma wait all morning,

stare out the window at the Cream of Wheat snowdrifts laying siege. We eat lunch (macaroni drowned in tomato soup and butter), get bundled up, and wade half a mile into the storm — the nor'easter setting on us, ripping and snarling, the way a pack of dogs'll set upon a deer come winter — over to Alma Anderson's.

Alma lets Ma use her phone to call Leon George, Granite's chief of police. Ma tells him Bub's run off. Alma and her husband are real nice to us, give us cocoa (Marshmallow Fluff scumming the top) and some Christmas cookies shaped like snowmen, angels, and wreaths. Leon calls about an hour later and says he's found Bub at the Legion hall, half crocked and saying that he ain't never going home again till he's good and ready. He's still sitting there, for all I know.

So, about ground into the yard like a cigarette butt, I thought about Bub and Frank — all the shit I'd taken — and everyone else my goddamned mother'd ever spread her legs for. I burned all that hate into my left arm — Frank always forgot I was lefty — and I let it grow and swell the way the mosquitoes did on me and Denny's arms when we was kids.

I caught Frank flush under the chin (swear I lifted him off the ground) and heard the *snick* of his neck snapping back. His eyes rolled up into his head, and Frank Sargent fell backwards onto the ground.

3

THE TREES in Cedar Swamp soared towards heaven the way no New Hampshire tree has a right, knitting a leafy roof that about snuffed the sun. But there were tree-free marshes, too, where the berries — raspberries, huckleberries, blueberries, blackberries, bayberries, and strawberries — thrived and deer held their town meetings. And there was Center Marsh in Cedar's heart — a stretch of half lake, half swamp that was a throwback to some old, old time. Ragged black and gray stumps, at least a dozen mouthfuls of rotted teeth, poked up through the water. And come sunrise, a haze so thick quilted Center Marsh that you couldn't see it, only smell it, only hear the muffled fog noises: beavers slapping tail, the bellyflop of a leaping bass, turtles and snakes plopping in. Good fishing, too. On most lakes and ponds in Granite and New Falls you were lucky to catch two or three three-pound bass in a season. On Center Marsh, you threw back anything under four pounds.

Fishing pole slung over my shoulder, I was headed towards Center Marsh. T'hell with the factory.

Cool in the woods that time of day, between night and sunup. Cool the way a good cellar is in summer. Mist hugged the ground, swirled around the trees — a smoky stripper eddying through the woods. As I hiked deeper into the swamp, the air changed: first shrugging off the last hint of town and Route 49, then shedding the woods' sweetness — moss and fern and pine needles — to bare the musty smell of damp black earth and swamp gas.

◢

Ass-deep in water, Azalea Kelley sloshed from blueberry bush to blueberry bush, methodically strangling each one — the way a woman would who'd once spent seven years wringing chicken necks over to Bennett's Egg Farm — the berries waterfalling into the ten-gallon bucket strapped to her waist. Azalea was one of those heavyset country women who seemed like she hadn't been born, but instead had been found in some White Mountains pasture, poking up through the thin New Hampshire soil, a vein of weathered granite. The sagging flesh on her upper arms danced when she walked, and her breasts — suggestive of fleshy Thanksgiving vegetables: Hubbard and butternut squashes, pumpkins, gourds — slumbered upon her stomach. And even on the most brilliant, purest days of spring there was a sense of November gray about her. She was fall, but only after the trees were bones.

She'd keep some of the berries she picked — same with the rhubarb and wild grapes. But most of them would wind up at the grocery stores in town: Buzzell's, Hempel's Market, Marble's Superette.

It was Azalea, in a way, who taught me the swamp. I'd known of her for years, since that first week me, Ma, and Bub moved to Granite from Hampstead. We were renting over to the Rock Goose Turnpike, a beat-up wood-frame job with peeling paint and half a barn falling off it, and the outhouse pit needed cleaning — real bad.

It was one of those Augusts where the sun hung bloody in the sky and you couldn't but breathe in or breathe out without chowing down on dust. Couldn't go into that outhouse, either, for the gag-a-maggot stink of ripening shit. And even if you could stand the smell, the flies'd get you. Those flies — sitting there and sharpening their legs — they weren't no ordinary pansy house flies that dip their legs polite in your tomato soup. They were as big around as a wedding ring, looking about ready to ooze something somewhere, flecks of green speckling their black bodies, a green I'd only seen on dead fish.

Anyway, the outhouse needs cleaning. My old man, Bub, says he sure's hell ain't doing it. "I already put up with enough shit in my life," he says, "and I'll be good and goddamned if I'm going to put up with any more."

Me? All I worry about is whether the shit is deep enough to go over my head.

So Bub checks around town, and a couple days later — the smell's become downright surly — he tells us that he's found some "old coot-ette" who'll do the job for ten bucks and all the shit she can eat. Looks like Bub's going to piss his pants, he's laughing so hard at his own joke; me and Ma don't even crack a smile. No point in encouraging him.

Come Saturday morning, Azalea Kelley tramps into the dooryard and proceeds to excavate our shithouse.

Azalea was the town scavenger, a two-legged rat — the kind of woman who kept regular hours at the town dump when she wasn't working Cedar Swamp. She walked the town's roads, too, dragging a homemade sled behind her as she picked up beer bottles, acorns, and street meat: runover squirrels, porcupines, and woodchucks — even dogs and cats.

At seven in the morning you'd see her on Little River Road; at three in the afternoon, Route 49; at eight, out to

Robie's Road. A ghost dressed in faded blue overalls and a green T-shirt, a floppy straw hat bouncing on her head. Walking. Not in any special hurry, thinking through each step like it meant something. Ma claimed Azalea had "the traveling evils." And more than one Granite mother got her kids to mind her by saying, "If you ain't good, I'll give you to Azalea Kelley!"

That was the town Azalea. Out in Cedar Swamp, living in a shack that was no more than a box with one window and a door, she trapped beaver, muskrat, and fox, berried, farmed, fished — anyone buying fresh bass or trout or hornpout in Granite was most likely getting fish she'd caught. Come fall, she gathered pine cones, moss, fir boughs, and suchlike and made wreaths for the Christmas trade. It was only after she'd sucked as much as she could from Cedar that Azalea came forth from the swamp to pick dump and do odd jobs — like cleaning outhouses.

But what truly made Azalea's reputation in town were the snappers; for all its airs, Granite, New Hampshire, was still a town where folks had a taste for turtle stew.

Ask her about stalking snapping turtles, and Azalea'd just point to the scar on her arm that was the shape of an eight-inch diamond. Story goes that Azalea once chopped the head off a good-sized snapper, a fifty-pounder, and when she bent over to slit up the rest, the turtle's head — its razor beak still clacking — somehow muckled ahold of her arm. Folks say a snapper can keep on biting for a full day after it and its head part company.

"Snapper's a prick," my Grandpa Ora told me. "Hardest beast in the world to kill; harder'n a man. Cut the heart out'n that bastard, bake it in the sun of an afternoon, and it'll still be beating at sundown. Gotta have yourself an extra pair when you decide you're gonna get yourself a snapper."

Azalea sure as hell had what it took. Long as there weren't any ice, she laid her traps, baited with rotting perch and kibbies, and hefted her ax — taking dead aim at turtle neck.

When I think on Azalea Kelley, though, I always remember a summer night I spent in Cedar Swamp:

The moon hangs in the sky as full as a Gonyer girl's pregnant belly. In the center of Linehan's Clearing someone's outlined a bandstand-sized circle with candles. Someone, or something, heaves from the other end of the clearing but pauses at the edge to listen and sniff, the way a deer will before it crosses open pasture. After a few seconds, the shadow moves again. Slow. Heavy.

Azalea slips into that candled circle, undresses. But not in a hurried way, not the way you would if you were going skinny dipping; she sheds her clothes in the lazy, ritual way that long-time lovers have. The freeing of each button, the unhooking of each clasp, is deliberate, holds meaning. She drops to all fours, her pumpkin breasts teasing the earth, and she licks the ground, grazes on the sweet, black swamp. She plunges her hands into the ground, works them in like a taproot in search of water till she's up to her elbows in dirt. She falls forward, butt twitching and toes wriggling, burying her face in the earth, moving it back and forth like she's washing in a brook. She pumps her arms up and down, up and down, thrusts her hips. Skinny tender roots dance up out of the ground and hug Azalea closer. They lace her body, pull her down, and she bucks, rocks harder. It seems I can smell the sweat beading on her body, hear her moans as she moves on the earth — just as much a creature of the swamp as a snapping turtle.

The town'd leaned on Azalea, demanded she make good on promises sealed by relatives who'd been long dead when she was born. These weren't the rickety promises of common folk, but the silent, yet understood, vows that pass among the "good" families in a small town. But Azalea couldn't deliver, even though she'd been born to the center-of-town Kelleys (the ones who ran the heating-oil business) and grown up in one of the black-shuttered, white Colonials that picketed the Plains — Granite's town green. She didn't marry, and by the time she was twenty-five she'd moved out of her parents' house and taken on a sagging saltbox over to Cheney's Boulevard. From there, she scuttled to Pickpocket Road to Robie's Road to Meeks Road. Each time, she moved farther from the Plains and closer to the swamp, which she'd taken to years before the way girls she'd gone to school with had taken to the PTA, church suppers, and the Avon lady.

Finally, instead of yielding to the gentle rounding of age and town life, she gave herself up to the swamp and the wrestling with snappers: Granite's crazy lady, who'd sprouted whiskers that stubbled her chin like winter cornstalks.

I understood what drew Azalea to the swamp. There'd been days when I'd wanted to steal away and lose myself there permanent. But I'd seen too much running away in my time, and the thought of it curdled my stomach.

Even so, after me and Mary Tucker broke up I retreated into the swamp, sought comfort in that wild womb. I wanted to get as far away as I could from the Plains, where Mary lived with her widowed mother. I needed to go where I could kill my blues, lay them to rest. That's the way it'd always been between Cedar Swamp and me.

Me and Mary'd gone together for almost two years, and I guess her mother'd seen enough. Bad enough that her only child — daughter of the Honorable Sanborn Bakie Tucker V — was probably "doing it," but she had the poor taste to be screwing Bub and Norma Duston's boy, Earl, who lived in a shack over on that Meeks Road.

So Mrs. Tucker got Mary into the Phillips Academy down to Exeter — Mary was *that* smart — and she had no choice but to go. We broke up before Mary even went away to school; Mrs. Tucker's faith in private education had been justified.

Sometimes I think Mary liked me because of — not in spite of — the shack and all. I was smart and tough, she said, and that made me seem less of a boy in her eyes. But the town — and her mother — had leaned on Mary the same as it'd leaned on Azalea. But, me aside, Mary Tucker hadn't been no budding swamper. She wasn't about to give up the Plains, her family's Colonial built in 1686, not for some high school boyfriend anyways. And, to be honest, I didn't blame her.

When I was a kid, folks in town lumped Azalea in with Alden Hartford's son, Lloyd, and Moses (Granite's Moses, I mean, not the Holy Bible's), which was wrong. Moses and Lloyd — Lloyd anyways — were simple. Azalea'd run off and maybe seemed simple because she spent so much time alone; but your lips'd move by themselves, too, if you spent 365 days a year in Cedar Swamp.

Now don't go thinking that I grew up in a town raunchy with retards and mental cases. It's just that when you're a kid those are the people who leave an impression. There's no way I could ever forget someone like Lloyd Hartford:

I'm seven years old, and Lloyd, who's three times my age, stands out to the Granite-Lamprey town line — near Mallory's Fruit & Real Estate — about every day and waves like he means it at the cars going by. Big, slow waves, like the pendulum on the Regulator clock that hangs in Hempel's Market. Alden drops him off at seven in the morning, picks him up at four. When he isn't waving at the cars, a wide smile on his Silly Putty face, Lloyd pretends to smoke sticks; always has a stack with him.

He shoves a cigar-thick stick in his mouth, puffs hard, takes it out, flicks away an imaginary ash (sometimes snapping off the tip of the stick), takes another drag. He's a real snooty smoker, his chin pointing towards the clouds and his stick held with his pinky pointing dainty.

Coming back from the dump one day, me and Bub drive by Lloyd. I ask Bub what makes Lloyd the way he is; why's he wave at the cars all day long? And Bub — I can tell he doesn't know what to say — says, "His old man did something bad to his ma when she was pregnant that made him into a retard. I'll tell you about it when you get older."

Even at that age, I know Bub is full of it. But I let it drop. A retard's woes ain't worth a smack in the face.

Moses held forth upon St. Laurent's Boulder, which was about the size of a two-room shack and situated in the crook of St. Laurent's elbow, a wicked sharp curve over to the Hutchins Road. In the winter of 1953, Emile St. Laurent stove up three different cars by skidding into that wall of granite. Third time, Emile broke his fool neck and died.

No one knew where Moses come from, and no one tried to find out. Me and Denny couldn't stay away from him. We snuck over to the Hutchins Road every chance we got to spy on him. Denny was crazy for Moses, said he learned more from Moses than he ever did from any teacher. When Denny said that, his eyes seemed just about ready to catch afire.

It's November — me and Denny are playing hooky from school — and Moses is preaching from St. Laurent's Boulder, shouting from the Old Testament. But he says the words flat, like they have no meaning or he doesn't know what he's saying: "And! all! the! waters! that! were! in! the! river! were! turned! to! blood!"

He picks through the Bible like he's picking dump, reads where his bony finger happens to fall as he riffles the pages: "All! darkness! shall! be! hid! in! his! secret! places! A! fire! not! blown! shall! consume! him!"

All the while, the black and gray rags that he wraps himself in flap in the sharp fall wind that tugs at his great dirty-white beard.

Sometimes he stands out there, back plank-straight, for twenty, thirty hours at a whack — whether it's ninety-five in the shade or twenty below. But he doesn't look human no more, looks like something out of a picture Bible. Parts of his face have melted away, leaving hollows and gullies that must fill with rainwater. And his hands are impossible gnarled — olden roots ripped from the earth. He's enough to make me start believing on the Bible again. Doesn't faze Denny, though.

"This'll get his attention," says Denny, who raises the BB gun and shoots Moses. He draws forehead blood. But Moses, who can't see us hiding across the road, doesn't flinch.

"The! young! lions! roared! upon! him! and! yelled! and! they! made! his! land! waste!"

Denny says, "Look at him, will ya. He don't even know we're here."

"Denny!" I whisper.

I don't have the stomach for this. I can see that Moses is rubbing Denny wrong, bringing out the mean in him the way you can rub certain baseball cards with a dime and uncover a hidden picture. It ain't funny no more. There's nothing funny about this hairy old man screeching from the Old Testament on a back road in an Old Testament town, his unbearable red blood spattering the yellowed pages of his Bible.

"Denny! Stop it!"

He shoots again; red pinpricks blossom on Moses' cheeks. "Guy's pissing me off," Denny says. He moves from the cover of the bushes, crosses the road, stands at the bottom of the boulder, and steadies the gun on Moses.

"The! fire! consumed! their! young! men!"

Denny stares hard at him — the way someone who can barely read will stare at the page of a book — then he starts to laugh like he knows something that me and Moses don't. Laughs even harder when Leon George, Granite's chief of police, pulls up in the cruiser; I'm laughing, too, but it's the kind of laughing that if it was sweat it'd stink bad.

Ain't nobody in town doesn't respect Leon George. To the men he's a brother, to the women a gentleman, and to the kids a father. He gets out of the cruiser and looks silent at us, kills the laughing damned quick. His look says, I'm pretty disappointed in you boys. Pretty disappointed. He sticks out his bear trap of a hand and Denny gives him the gun — it's a Daisy, too. Leon opens the cruiser's back door, meaning we should get in.

As I slide in, I look back at Moses, half expect him to somehow acknowledge us. A wink, maybe. A nod. Nothing, except the words — spoken in another language, Moses' language: "Thou! art! my! hiding! place! and! my! shield! I! hope! in! thy! word!"

By the time I was fifteen, Lloyd Hartford's old man'd died and Lloyd's uncles put him away over to Concord. And Moses? Moses didn't mount St. Laurent's Boulder one spring morning, and no one's seen him since. They haven't looked, either.

About a quarter mile from where Azalea was berrying I bushwhacked some twenty feet off the path to where clumps of mushrooms grew close together in the black earth. I kneeled, spit into my right hand — picked that up from Frank — and drove it into the ground, my fingers clawing at the musty soil; I pictured Azalea again in Linehan's Clearing.

I pulled free, clutching a clump of earth that wriggled with nightcrawlers, the plump, moist worms looking like limp spikes or spare fingers. I dumped them, dirt and all, into a cookie tin.

I pushed off onto Center Marsh in Azalea's rowboat, oaring strong but smooth on glassy water; we had an understanding: I always left part of my catch for her.

Swamp spooked me some. And at that time of day, when the mist spooled off the swamp and swirled and whirled like hundreds of ghosts dancing on the water, burning up before the rising sun, that feeling grew even stronger. It was more than being alone, of being just another swamp animal on the marsh. It was the oldness. The swamp was so old, a place that'd never caught up, a place where a humongous prehistoric beast could still rear up out of the ooze, claws and teeth bared, its bellow echoing all the way to the Plains, where everyone would stop for a second, then think it was just the B & M roaring through. And the stumps and slivers of trees poking through the water, the muffled noises — a place where things happened that no one ever knew about. A good place to die.

As I rowed, I daydreamed: a body floats face down; sun scales the sky; the ringing hymn of the water bugs; fish snuffle the body; snapper rips free a hank; the body sinks, weightlessly cartwheeling its way deep into the watery black . . .

The heron burst from the swamp grass, and I fell over backwards in the boat and whacked my head.

Even after that heron — shitpokes is what we called 'em

— flapped away, my breath was still trapped in my chest and I could hear my heart pound. In the withered mist the bird seemed no more than an undigested chunk of dream flushed from cover by accident. But it'd been real, all right: I had the goose egg to prove it. I hoped that the shitpoke'd been at least half as scared as I'd been.

Midmorning. I shut my eyes, felt the sun work my bare back, smiled at the tingling. Still. Trees onshore stiff, the water like fresh rink ice. The high-pitched hum of the water dancers started, stopped; started, stopped.

I grabbed a crawler out the tin, pinched it between my thumb and forefinger for a few seconds, watching it fight; it sure was game. I speared it on the hook, doubled it over, and speared it again; I thought of Mr. Cole telling us in sixth grade that worms have ten hearts. My fingers tasted like dirt where I'd held it. I raised my pole, brought it back over my head, then flicked it forward: the reel singing soft, the line arching, then the *plop* of hook, crawler, and bobber. The best casts — the moving in two different directions in one graceful motion — were like watching a good second baseman complete a double play. I yawned, watched the red and white bobber rise, fall. The sun climbed — " 'Nother hot one," I imagined Billy at the factory saying — but it still looked young and light yellow, giving no hint of how hateful it'd be by noon. I stared at the bobber, the water stippling at less than a breeze, holding my pole loose. I sighed, reeled in. Crawler still on the hook, still struggling, not so dark no more — mud-puddle brown. I cast again, another double-play ball, the reel sang, and hook, crawler, and bobber hit the water again . . . then were gone.

I jerked the line tight, bringing up the pole, burying the

hook in the fish's mouth. I reeled hard, balancing the line between the tight and the slack. And right there, that's the sweet moment when you're fishing — when one foot is propped against the side of the boat, your back is bowed slight, and the only thing in the world is the heavy, firm weight tugging at the other end of the line.

I could've sit like that all day long.

◢ 4

"MALLORY'S watermelons, they'd been asking for it."

That's what Denny told the cops. But that's getting ahead of the story.

You see, Freddy Mallory — owner of the melons in question — was one of Granite's part-time cops, and he'd been on Denny's ass two months running. Mallory'd pulled Denny over five times "for suspicion of driving while under the influence." Twice he'd ransacked Denny's 'vette "under suspicion of the transportation of illegally expropriated goods." Now Denny drank and Denny thieved, but he wasn't numb.

Plus, Mallory kept on stopping by Denny's house "just to shoot the shit" with Denny's old man. And it seemed Denny couldn't but look in his rearview mirror and there'd be Mallory in the Chevy cruiser, some three telephone poles back — porculent bastard.

"Just keeping you close to the bag," Mallory told Denny. "Close to the bag."

What made it even worse, though, is that Mallory was one of those guys who figured that packing a gun added at least a foot to his dick. Pussle-gutted prick used to strut around town with his chest puffed out and his arms hung just so.

It wasn't like he needed the money or nothing. He owned Mallory's Fruit & Real Estate out on Route 49 near the Granite-Lamprey line. The store had been a garage once, but Mallory'd done his damnedest to quaint up the place. Got himself a sign painted that showed a straw-hatted boy burying his freckled face in a canoe-sized hank of watermelon. He'd slapped on a big ol' country porch that was a farmer's jungle of butter churns, weather vanes, washboards, milking stools, and the like — couldn't but turn around without whanging your head on the clutches of Indian corn or the varnished gourds that hung from the raw beams. Then there were the Granite postcards and T-shirts and towels and mugs; little plastic outhouses that when you opened the door that same cute straw-hatted kid would piss on you; velvet paintings of the Plains, the town hall, and the seminary, which'd burned in '57; sawtooth-edged cardboard signs that said: "The More I Cook the Behinder I Get," "Granite: The Center of the Universe," and (for the bathroom door) "Sshh!! I Think I Hear a Moose Snorting."

Mallory's workers had to wear shit-kickers and dungaree overalls and say "yessir" and "no, ma'am" as they peddled all that fresh *New Hampshire* produce trucked up to Mallory's from Lawrence, Massachusetts, and other points south. And Mallory's office out back, where he now and again turned on us and sold off pieces of Granite to the Mass-holes who wanted more than sweet corn, summer squash, and a T-shirt to remember New Hampshire by.

Mallory sold gravestones out back, too. Granite stones as shiny and black as snake eyes. The town had been famous once for that ornery black rock; but it'd been mined out a long time ago, and the quarries had given in to water. Anyone who was anybody in town got laid to rest under black granite, the only kind Mallory sold. The common dead had to make do with gray granite or even nothing at all.

Only thing left from Mallory's Fruit & Real Estate's days as a gas station were the old-fashioned, bubble-topped pumps out front. They must've been something special, too, because Mallory charged ten cents a gallon more for gasoline than anybody else in town.

But Mallory's watermelons lured us. They were watermelons with a reputation. Mallory bragged about them the way the father of seven daughters brags. Most folks in town wouldn't have bought shit from Freddy Mallory, but they came from miles around to buy his watermelons. They were *that* good. Those watermelons held the sweetest, softest, pinkest melon meat I ever tasted — melted on your tongue like cotton candy — and the sticky juice almost tasted better than a cold beer on a hot day. Mallory wouldn't say where he got his melons — some people said he grew 'em out to Cedar Swamp, but I knew that was bullshit — but come summer there they'd be, hundreds (maybe even thousands) stacked outside his fruit stand like so many pregnant bellies.

Three in the morning: me, Denny, Stain, and Dog stood in Mallory's parking lot, checking out the watermelons. We weren't quite sure how we'd ended up at Mallory's. All we knew is that, like most days, we'd started out at Swett's Pond.

◢

We killed so many afternoons over to Swett's Pond early that summer that it's hard to separate one from the other, like trying to husk corn before its time. Looking back, I see days so rich in signs and portents that some moments have taken on the power of dreams. Looking back.

There was a sameness, too, though: the heat, the dying afternoon light, the beer.

Beer: brew, suds, oil, hooters, cold ones, Bosco, and, when warm, skunk piss. Sweaty bottles, cans so cold your tongue stuck to 'em, 'Gansett's Giant Imperial Quarts. We passed judgment on Granite's grocery stores based solely on the coldness of their beer. Buzzell's beer, this side of freezing, went down best; you could fingernail ice from Buzzell's bottles — the icy shavings curling, melting on your hand — and that first beer'd burn winter as it slid down. Drink, damn didn't we drink. Couldn't do nothing without a beer in hand. Nothing. Even taking a leak we had a beer in tow. I suppose that said it all: the beer gurgling in one end and whizzing out the other, one of those vicious cycles. All that beer money, pissed away.

Every Friday and Saturday we got drunk: crocked, loaded, shit-faced, feeling good, stewed, horse-ified, lit up, stiffer'n a board, in the bag, bombed, the works. Something made me crave to drink come sundown Fridays and not stop till Sunday morning; and praise the Lord for hypocrites that you can't buy beer in New Hampshire before noon on Sundays. Don't know why we drank so. You'd a thought I could've figured out what was what. But it was like I took one hard look at Bub and Ma and Frank and decided to make every goddamned mistake they ever made and then some. I knew them and their lives, tasted their sorrows; but I just didn't get it.

Ma'd get wicked pissed at me. She could go honky-tonking and get boozed. But not me. One Saturday night, figuring to learn me a lesson, she rearranged my room. I staggers in late that night in the dark and I go to flop on my bed. Except it ain't there no more. I smack my face on the floor and fall asleep in a puddle of nose blood.

Anyway, Swett's Pond was where you'd most likely find us late of an afternoon. But before I start in on me, Denny, and everyone else, let me tell you about the pond.

Some ten minutes from the Plains, Swett's Pond lay a ways down the road from the red chicken coops of Bennett's Egg Farm. The pond was one of our secret places. The same as outsiders didn't know the best stands to lay for deer or the best pools to cast for trout, they didn't know about Swett's Pond. It was understood — from the high Kelleys to the low Gonyers (we Dustons stood somewhere at the bottom of the second division with the Gonyers) — that we'd keep it that way; secrets bind a place like Granite.

You couldn't see the pond from the road. You had to know it. Some after Bennett's you pulled over, stepped out, and walked a path that, from the road, looked like any other. But after a hundred yards or so that path opened out onto a hill that guarded a small beach and a pond, which wasn't so big that you couldn't swim across it, but if you did you hurt some. We collected there after work, bushwhacking in as mothers and their sticky, sunburned kids headed out.

Like I said, the afternoons at Swett's Pond ran together. But there were times that summer when, maybe for a few seconds, our small world, for whatever reasons, seemed to stand still. Those moments I remember best:

Stain's talking, picking up steam, waving his hands, trying his damnedest to convert us.

"This is how I see it," he says, popping a Schlitz. "Got me a 'sixty-one Fairlane right now. Ain't no reason why I can't fix that bastard up nice and trade up to a — oh, I don't know — a 'sixty-two Falcon. See, I'm already ahead of the game right there. Then I take that Falcon, do the same thing, and maybe snag me a 'sixty-three Impala. Way I figure, I keep churning 'em over like that, and in five years I'm driving me a brandy-new Caddy. Damn right. Got to keep trading up."

Who can argue with that?

"Sometimes I wish the war hadn't a ended," Denny says. "My bother Brian says there ain't nothing better than Nam-style poontang."

"Yeah," I say. "Your brother the dick-head."

"I'm serious," Denny says. "Vietnam War don't end, maybe I get out of this shithole town."

"Blow it out your ass, Gamble," Dickie says. "What did you wanna do? End up like Wally George?"

Wally George, the poor bastard, was the only Graniter killed in Vietnam. Couple of years ahead of us in school, he signed up the day after graduation the way other kids got married. I know it was longer, but it seemed only a week'd gone by before he got shipped back to us — horizontal. His father, Chief of Police Leon George, said a sniper took him. But there'd been a story going round that Wally'd been balling some booby-trapped whore and got his ass blown up. Sounded like bullshit, but you never know. Anyways, across from the fire station the town'd planted a black granite cross and chiseled his name on it.

"I don't know," Denny says, shrugging. "I wouldn't mind getting me one of those fancy granite gravestones."

We're sitting on the beach, shooting the shit, hoisting a few, when Kevin Moreau walks-slides down the hill towards us. Denny tenses, arm veins filling. Kevin's deepset eyes are the size of steel-drum covers and he's so skinny he casts no shadow; puckerbrush hair scrapes his waist.

"Denny, uh, man, I'm, uh, um," Kevin says. "I really, uh, need, um."

He stalls, kicks it over one more time. "Hash, Denny. Uh, hash." Stalls again.

Denny won't look at us. We all know he sells dope, has been known to break into a house. But we don't talk about it, and we're past trying to take Denny Gamble in hand — not that it ever worked.

But Kevin Moreau's standing there — in front of us, his brothers — shames Denny. And finally he turns his animal eyes on Kevin and says, "Get the fuck out of here."

Denny and me swim lazy out to the raft — long, slow strokes that barely ripple the water. Even so, when we hitch ourselves out of the pond and onto the raft, Denny sucks greedy for air: his lips are blue-ing, his chest heaves hard.

When we were kids, we ran each other into the ground every day.

"My fucking word."

Denny points to the far end of the beach, where Pam Durocher and Stain have — hand in hand — just stepped out of the woods. The good news is in Stain's walk.

"Stain?" Dickie says. "Stain Thistle?"

I shake my head. Denny and Pam broke up only a couple weeks ago. Denny told me she's pregnant.

◢

Anyways, we'd managed somehow to drive to Mallory's Fruit & Real Estate from Swett's Pond — four of us wedged into Denny's 'vette — without getting ourselves killed. Now when a bunch of guys are about to do a fool thing, there comes a point it can slide either way. Someone can say, "Damn, what if we get picked off by the cops?" Then everyone gets deflated, and the nervous giggles set in. Before you know it, you're all back in the car laughing like friggin' jackasses about what almost was. That's where we were at as we stood in Mallory's parking lot, wild drunk on beer and the backwash of a hot summer's night.

"Fuck you guys waiting on?" said Denny, whipping out his jackknife.

He picked out a melon — fussy as an old lady — then, real careful, cut a hole in one end about as big around as a Schonland frank. Me, Dog, and Stain looked at each other, back at Denny, then at each other again — he ain't really going to do *that,* is he — grinning at the inevitability of it all as Denny dropped his dungarees, shoved his Big Willie up inside that watermelon, and proceeded to woo it.

"Don't you go looking at me like that," Denny said. "Get your own."

Stain laughed first, small hiccups (the first time turning over that old Ford pickup that's been wintering out to the barn) that shook his body like that same pickup bucking its way up Rockrimmon Road to the fire tower. When Denny started sliding that melon up and down, up and down, and sighing love noises, Dog couldn't hold back no more. He dropped to his knees, soundless laughs earthquaking his gut, twisting his face. I laughed hard, too — pants-pissing caliber. We were like three happy 'tards escaped from the nut house up to Concord. And when Denny flipped me the jackknife and said, "Gentlemen, synchronize your dicks," I grabbed my stomach and rolled onto the ground like I was trying to keep my guts from dribbling out.

So there we were, the four of us sitting up against Mallory's porch, mounting watermelons at three in the morning. You know, it didn't feel half bad — for a fruit, I mean — kind of warm and mooshy. And that's how Freddy Mallory and Leon George found us when they pulled up in the cruiser. The evidence sat upright on our rapidly withering rods as the cruiser's spastic blue lights nailed us to the spot like we was jacked deer.

"What you doing to my melons?" Mallory squealed as he ran-waddled towards us. "Fuck you doing? You little homos! Stop screwing my watermelons! You let go of 'em! Jesus H. Christ!"

We didn't need much coaxing. We plucked those melons off our dicks like they was infested with the Seabrook radioactive cock-rot. Well, me, Dog, and Stain did, anyway. Denny still pumped at his melon like a stray tom in heat.

"You filthy little bastard," Mallory squeaked. "You let go of my watermelon."

Denny said, "Be thankful it ain't your wife, lard-ass."

You could tell that one part of Mallory wanted to trample Denny Gamble and rip that goddamned watermelon off him — cock and all. But some squeamishness stalled him. He stood there, squirming — a little boy who has to take a leak bad but whose old man's been on the can for at least half an hour. Leon, arms folded, slouched against the cruiser.

Finally, Mallory blurted, "You shut your mouth, Denny Gamble!"

Denny closed his eyes, thrust harder at the melon, and moaned, "Oh, Freddy. My Fat Freddy."

"Stop it!" Mallory ordered. "Stop it!"

Denny didn't. And that's when I saw some twelve-year-old kind of Freddy Mallory. In school they'd called him Porky, snorted hog grunts when he hove by. Bet they snapped his pink ass with rat-tailed towels, greased his jock with Atomic Balm, and hung him by his belt from the clothes hooks in the boys' locker room. Poor little Porky Mallory — what an a-hole.

"Stop," Mallory said again.

Denny — melon-frenzied — paid him no mind.

Slow, deliberate, each muscle in his arm working, Mallory drew his gun, raised it, and, with two hands, held it on Denny. We froze, the way a mouse will when the kitchen light clicks on at four in the morning. A snap of fear even shivered through Denny.

"Stop, goddamn you, or I'll shoot."

That's when Leon George planted himself between Denny Gamble and Freddy Mallory's gun and sent Mallory back to the cruiser.

We paid for the watermelons. And Leon, good egg that he was, gave us a talking-to, then let us go. As Leon and Mallory drove off, Denny said, "Know that first one I did? Plugged up the hole in that sucker and stuck it back in the stack. I ain't got no idea where it is."

The next day Leon told Mallory to turn in his badge and gun, told him he couldn't use him no more.

◢ 5

AWAKE. Cotton mouth, head pissing and moaning. Even with the window open my room was bloated with that heavy heat seems it'll smother you, the carnival fat lady sitting on your face. I looked out the window — leaves stiff, sun dishwater-dull — figured it to be about eight. I wanted, needed, more sleep. But that Sunday morning smell of bacon and pancakes frying had worked its way up from downstairs. My mouth watered, tongue ached. Sometimes there's nothing better than good food. Nothing. I threw back my sweat-soaked sheet, plodded to the top of the stairs.

"Ma! I'll be right down!"

"Okay."

In the bathroom, I hefted the pail of clean water and filled the sink half. Weren't much of a bathroom: a sink with a pail full of scummed water under it, a chipped enamel slop bucket that smelled like it needed emptying, and a mirror on the door that rubbered up your face when you looked in it. Three thin towels, rougher than an old rooster's skin, hung on tenpenny nails driven into the bare beams. I took a deep breath and plunged my head into the piss-warm water I'd poured.

Frank and Ma sat at the kitchen table, eating. Frank had shaved (a once-a-week event) and slicked down what little hair he had left with Brylcreem; I'd know that barber shop smell anywhere. Ma wore a plain blue dress she'd bought for half a buck at Goodwin's flea market the Sunday before. They looked almost happy sitting there, wearing their clean clothes, drinking black coffee. But they were tired. Not the staying-up-late or working-too-hard tired, but the other kind. The tired where the way you live wears you down like the eraser on a pencil; in the end, all that's left is a dirty stub. That kind of tired.

"Sonuvabitch if that don't smell good, Ma," I said. "I'm so hungry I could eat the asshole out of a skunk."

"Plate's on the stove," she said.

I couldn't wait to lay into that heap of bacon and pancakes. Soon as I sat down I lathered the cakes up with Land O' Lakes butter, then drowned them and the bacon in Vermont Maid syrup. Frank poured me coffee.

"This is real good," I said. "Where'd you get the bacon?"

"Frank helped Roland Simes put in a fence couple days ago," Ma said. "He give us a whole bunch of meat. This is from those pigs he slaughtered last year."

"Yut," Frank said, nodding. "Nice of Roland."

"How's he doing?" I asked. "Ain't seen him in a coon's age."

Frank sipped on his coffee, said, "Heat's raising hell with his chickens. Ain't laying worth a damn. Some of 'em's dying on him right in the chicken coop. Just keeling over."

"Sucks," I said.

"Heat's awful," Ma said. "What's it, been like this almost two weeks now? Ain't right."

"Roland was telling me that over to Manchester they found three old people dead in their apartments because they was too hot and didn't have no good air," Frank said. "Heat's a prick."

"Ought to try working at the barrel factory," I said.

"It's enough to make you crazy," Ma said. "It's weather like this people start doing crazy things. You watch. Heat gets in your head, makes you like that Dirty Willy."

"Come on, Ma," I said. "Who told you that?"

"You watch," she said. "You just watch."

"Why don't you just screw it, go back north?" I asked Frank. "You don't like it here no more."

"Don't know," he said.

I shrugged; I didn't know neither.

" 'S hard to leave something you made with your own two hands," he said, meaning the shack. "Could never build nothing like this now."

"Y'ain't happy."

"There's worse."

We rested on the dusky porch — two dogs panting quiet — trying to reel in the breeze that'd sprung up after sundown. Some nights we sat out there till bedtime, nursing beers, watching night fall, deepen. We listened to the peepers set the night air to shimmying, to the low honk of the bullfrog, to the gentle but sure voice — like a minister's — of Ned Martin as he described the Red Sox game on the radio. At those times, when me and Frank were caught in the spell of the night swamp and the ballgame, it almost seemed we could be father and son. There's times when fathers and sons don't need nothing more than to be together, hypnotized by the same things, the son learning what's worth heeding, what isn't. His porch on a summer's night was Frank's gift to me.

He lit a Camel, coughed — a wet, rattling cough that shook his body so hard that he set his beer down; hand to mouth, he bent double like someone'd pulled him to the floor by the hair. When it passed, he walked to the screen door, opened it, hawked, then spit. He stared into the night, drawing on his Camel so that the orange glowed brighter.

"When I was a kid," he said, "not much older'n you, I drove truck for some small-assed oil outfit upcountry. What was it? Shit, can't even remember the name. Anyways, me and Floyd Watkins was their only drivers. Tells you how big a outfit it was."

He paused, coughed again. Short this time.

"Well, me and Floyd was like this," Frank said, holding up two fingers side by side. "Thicker'n shit. Did everything together. Drink — boy, did we drink — hunted, fished, chased pussy. Raised as much hell as you could upcountry in those days.

"We'd always head out together in the mornings to make our deliveries. One January morning I'm behind him and we're probably driving too fast. We were in the middle of the January thaw and the roads are always slick in the morning from the water freezing the night before. Anyways, we're driving and giving each other the finger and making faces at each other, carrying on like real assholes, when Floyd's truck hits an ice patch and skids towards the guardrails. He can't straighten her out — the truck isn't that big, no big tanker or nothing, but it's big enough — and it smacks the rails hard, slices right through 'em, and it's a long ways down.

"I fishtail to a stop and I runs to the side of the road. His rig is falling and falling, rolling down the 'bankment through the snow like a kid throwed off his toboggan. One long drop. And I'm just praying she don't blow. But she does. Blows all to hell. I swear I didn't hear her go; just saw the fire shoot up, the truck cave in.

"But it wasn't the accident that got me so much. I mean, I was tore up about it; but what're you going to do? It was when he was headed towards those guardrails. Just before he hit, I got one last look at him in his side mirror. And you know, that bastard wasn't fighting that wheel or trying to straighten her out or anything. All he does is look up and wave at me."

"Suicide?" I said.

"No, goddammit! No! You ain't listening. I told you he hit ice, lost control. But there, at the end, he just give up. That's all. He give up. Thought I knew him. But the bastard just up and quit."

"Uh-huh."

"Understand?"

Frank dropped his Camel on the floor, heeled it out, shook his head. "Can't believe he give up."

He fired up another smoke. "Just remember, Earl, there's worse than not being happy."

6

JOHNSON had stuck me on the burner, and I was unloading paint drums from Phil's trailer truck. I'd pulled about a hundred drums, and my sweat shivered me as it slithered from my armpits. I tugged at a drum, letting it thud down, and rolled it to the trailer's mouth. When I'd done nine or ten like that I trudged — our knee-high, rubber boots were made for trudging — up to the mouth and dropped the drums to Dog, running the burner.

When you're doing jackass work — unloading a truck, say — it helps if you can keep yourself company. What I mean is that some guys can't stand to work lonely; they need to shovel the bull back and forth. Dickie was like that. He'd rather grow a hernia working with someone else on a hard job than do some tit job by himself. Me, I never had that problem. I'd rather bullshit with myself anyways; you learn those kinds of things when you're brought up the way I was.

If you could've seen me working you might've thought I'd gone simple, maybe caught Dirty Willy Disease. I kept smiling off and on, almost laughing sometimes, because I couldn't keep the sight of Denny humping Freddy Mallory's watermelons out of my mind; I figured me, Denny, Stain, and Dog'd still be talking about that night when we were ninety. Already, it was one of our legends, something we could grab on to, something that belonged to us.

But Denny and the melons dredged up Mallory's lard-soaked carcass, too. And chewing over what Mallory almost did made my balls crawl. Looking to shed Mallory, I thought on his daughter instead.

Kate Mallory, like Mary Tucker and Azalea Kelley, had been born to the Plains' center-of-town Colonials. But it'd never seemed to impress her too much, not the way it had Mary. Kate, in fact, had moved out of her old man's house that spring and taken a place way over on Britton Road. Me and Kate'd been friends in school, though nothing had really come of it, me and Mary being a steady thing and all. But the question had always been tucked away as to what it'd be like to fuck Freddy Mallory's daughter. I yanked down another drum, letting it drop on top of my steel toes.

The truck driver usually helped unload. That way you saved all that gallivanting back and forth. But while I busted balls, Phil wet-dreamed away in the truck's cab, Yankees cap pulled low — not even the decency of a Red Sox cap — and a dog-eared copy of *Hustler* draped over his crotch. Phil was the kind of dink who'd tap his cigar ash on your arm on purpose, then wink like he was letting you in on some joke.

Dog snipped the bolts that bound steel rings to the drums, flipped the rings to one side (to be sanded and painted later) and the covers to the other. He wheeled the drums to the burner, where he turned them upside down — some of those bastards were heavy, too — onto the steel track that creaked through the furnace. The drums dripped red, yellow, and blue paint into a trough that ran the length of the burner — a chemical brook we called the pit, same as we called under the blaster the pit; sometimes we even called the whole damned factory the pit.

After a couple more trips, sick of breathing in the chemical but relish-sweet smell deep in the truck, I said, "Man, I've had enough," and I jumped down, the pink muck sucking at my boots.

"Dog," I said, "it's your turn up in that goddamned sweatbox."

"Here," he said, handing me a quart bottle of water so cold it hurt my teeth to drink it. But I inhaled about half anyways, letting it dribble down my chin, drinking so hard I about lost my breath. Dog threw off his gloves, hand-cleaned the bottle's mouth like I had rabies or something, and chugged the rest.

"What a fucking day," Dog said, swiping sweat from his forehead and leaving a black smudge.

"Y'say that every goddamned day," I said.

"Tell me it ain't so."

Work didn't come natural to Dog. Wasn't that he was lazy. He was just one of those guys made to fish, drink beer, and sleep. Sleep, could that man sleep. If we'd've let him, he wouldn't've ever got out of bed on weekends — 'cept to take a leak. I don't know how many times we stopped by his place at seven o'clock on a Saturday night — his mother rocking and knitting on the front porch — and had to haul his ass out of bed. He'd've been sleeping since the night before and it'd still take a freezing pail of well water to coax him awake. Slept at work, too: he'd curl up in a trailer-truck box, drop off on the can, snuggle with the gloves, boots, and hard hats in the storeroom. Andy found him hibernating under the blaster one day. On those days when he did manage to wake up there was a fifty-fifty chance that instead of coming to work he'd snag his rod and reel and a six-pack of Bud and lope on over to Spofford's Point, where he probably snoozed more than he fished. He had a permanent spot on Johnson's shit list, but the company wouldn't fire him. Johnson knew that Dog wanted to get canned so he could collect unemployment and finally get his rest. Johnson wasn't about to give him that; if Dog wanted out, he'd have to quit. So Dog did his time — working slower'n cold molasses goin' uphill in a thunder shower — stealing Zs whenever.

Already beat — wasn't even eleven yet — we leaned against the truck and stared at the barn-sized burner, its outer wall crusty with soot and rust, its stack burping black smoke. Everything began out there. Dirty drums were unloaded and fed to the burner, which, at twelve hundred degrees, fried most of the gunk. The air around the burner rippled with the heat, even in winter.

Dog sighed and crawled up into the truck. I grabbed a shovel and skimmed the scaly scum from the pit, flipping the black gobs of paint and chemicals into the holding tank back of the burner. That tank of poison got emptied once a week by an unmarked truck with Rhode Island plates, and I tried not to think too much about where that shit ended up. Sometimes I felt like I was poisoning my town. Not that Granite had given me a whole helluva lot. And I'd have to bury the fact deep in my gut, where some kind of scar tissue could seal it tight, that I didn't have the balls to quit the drum factory; that, somehow, my paycheck made it all right. There was a story going around the shop, though, that in May we'd gotten caught dumping that crap into Boston's sewers. At least they did it down there, over the border. Let the Taxachusetts Mass-holes who owned the drum factory shit in their own bed.

I tipped a couple drums onto the track and watched them get drawn into the roaring gas jets. Some paint drippings caught and drifted back my way, little rafts of fire. I scooped them out, stomped them the way you would the eggs in a den of snakes. You had to be careful, especially with paint drums. Just a speck of fire could touch off the pit and send a wave of flames rushing at the man running the burner. We'd had a couple guys get burned real bad; didn't get to the hose quick enough. One of those poor bastards, Kenny Mansfield, was still in the hospital down to Boston; been there going on ten months, with over seventy-five percent of his body burned up. Kenny was a numb fuck, but no man deserves that.

I lifted more drums onto the track, picking up the pace, falling into my work rhythm — and pissing Dog off no end.

"What the fuck you trying to prove, Duston?" he said. "You some kind of hero?"

I shrugged and kept working. I wasn't trying to show anybody up or nothing. It's just the way I am. No matter where I work, I give my bosses a good eight hours, and they goddamn well know it. Someone pays you regular, you don't beat the meat. You work. That's the way I was brought up. Hell, when my Grandma Jenny was sixty-seven years old she pushed so hard over to the shoe shop in Brentwood that she worked her twin sister, my Auntie Leah, out of a job and herself out of this world. Grandma Jenny slumped dead at the stitcher one February morning, her foot still jammed on the pedal that ran the machine, the coarse black thread sewing together the fingers on her fish-bone of a left hand. Tell you one thing, though. When I croak, my dead ass ain't going to be draped over no 55-gallon steel drum.

Dog started yelling, arguing with somebody. "There, you sonuvabitch!" he shouted. "How you like it?"

Holding a drum chest high, he banged it against the side of the truck. He shoved it a couple more times, bullying it.

"Cocksucker!"

He grunted the drum over his head — knees bent, back bowing — whung it off the truck, jumped down after it, and laid into it with his steel-toed boots, dimpling the steel.

"That'll learn ya! Miserable bastard!"

At least Dog wasn't taking his blues out on me; got enough of that at home.

Now it might seem that a man beating hell out of a steel drum ought to get sent up to the nut house in Concord. But I figure if a guy can cure what's ailing him by muckling ahold of a steel drum and teaching it a lesson, let him. Leave him be. He ain't drinking himself to death or beating up his girl or something. Tangling with a barrel ain't nothing. I wished Denny'd picked on steel drums instead of raising the kind of hell he did; I'd have stole 'em for him if he'd wanted 'em bad enough.

The drum, on its side now, rolled away from Dog, getting caked with the slime out to the burner. He dove at it, his chin clanging against the steel, arms wrapped wide around it like a groom trying to lug his four-hundred-pound woman over the threshold. They roiled and rocked in the acid slop, first Dog on top, then the drum, Dog hammering away and the drum rolling and rolling till the two of them got wedged against the factory — the drum on top, and Dog wriggling underneath.

"Get it off me!" Dog bellowed. "Get it off!"

I squished over, tugged the drum away. Dog looked up at me — the panic and frustration clearing — then looked down. "Gotta go bathroom," he mumbled.

Somehow, he stood up and slunk off without looking me in the eye. All he needed was a nap. After that nap he'd act like nothing ever happened, no yelling, no duking it out with the goods. That was both the good thing and the pain in the ass about Dog. Sleep was his eraser, making it easier for him to believe that beer and fishing were the only things that mattered.

Some minutes later, Johnson oozed out to the burner and asked, "What the fuck's the holdup?" I told him that the track'd gotten gummed up, needed cleaning.

"Well, get your ass in gear," he said and walked inside.

◢ 7

ROUTE 36 out of Manor Beach is sandwiched by a salt marsh. And across that marsh, over towards Seabrook, is where they was building the nuke plant. Backlit by pinkish floodlights that sicked up the night sky, the plant's black skeleton reared up out of the marsh; its towers spit fierce blue flame; and its girders and cranes stuck up in the air like the legs of so many dead mosquitoes. You could just hear the *stump-whump, stump-whump* of heavy machines laboring — fat men climbing the stairs — and barely see the starry pinpricks that were the welders. The whole state of New Hampshire had been carrying on over that plant for years. I didn't want it built, not that what I thought amounted to a piss hole in the snow, because it reminded me of the barrel factory, 'cept it was about a thousand times bigger. Figured there was no percentage in that.

"It's a sight, ain't it?" Denny said.

"Uh-huh," I said.

It was late at night — or early in the morning, depending on how you look at those kinds of things — and me and Denny were driving home from the beach. We were both half crocked, but I figured Denny should drive because I'd lost count at fourteen beers, and he'd only lost track at eleven. Windows down, we were doing a good ninety, ninety-five in Denny's 'vette. Cruising speed.

I slumped in my seat and watched the 'vette devour the road, saw the highway's white and yellow lines flicker as unstable as dreams. I stuck my head out the window and guzzled the night wind, which prickled my face and waved my hair. I wondered how Denny could drive. But his face, etched by the dashboard lights, set calm and steady. Every few seconds he would wince, like somebody was ratcheting his nuts, and hit the gas pedal harder; but that was Denny, you know, so I didn't give it much thought. No sound except for the rush of wind, the 'vette's bragging engine. Lots of guys blast their rock 'n' roll when they attack the road, but Denny never clicked on the radio. He had all the rock 'n' roll he needed right inside his head.

The red needle slid past 110. I didn't give a fuck. I trusted Denny, same as he trusted me. It'd been that way since we'd first laid eyes on each other in grammar school — instant brothers — and we'd never questioned it.

I suppose that speeding is a way of saying "screw you" to the world. But, numb as it sounds, it's also a way to be free — ask anyone with a hot car — and Denny liked to be freer than most. I pressed my foot to the floor, tromping on an imaginary gas pedal. Seemed any second we could take off. If only she'd go a little faster, a little faster — please. That was straight road, Route 36, a razor cut from Manchester to the ocean. Smooth and flat, it begged you to haul ass. Denny grinned at me, nodding his head. I grinned back. We didn't say much, no need. When you've been friends for as long as we'd been, and were drunk together, there wasn't much to say. We knew without saying, understood without explaining. Religion.

He grinned again, but mean this time. I couldn't see his

face clear, but I knew something was up. Drunk or not, I knew. He glanced at me, checked the speedometer, ran a hand back through his hair. A deep breath, like before diving into winter water.

He cut the lights and we were running dark.

We barrel-assed through shifting shades of black and shadow, speeding on a quilt layered with different swatches of black. Denny was the quilter who knew every stitch, knew where every thread went, knew what each patch of darkness meant. Shadows: the road the blackest shadow, the one we followed; the wild woods that menaced the road; the sky, lighter than the rest, shifting, changing, the stars snuffed, the moon swiped; and Denny's face — shadows flickered there, shadows of pain, cunning shadows — the dark laugh hidden in the corners of his eyes.

Denny reached under his seat and pulled out a six of Budweiser cans. He popped two of 'em, the piss-warm beer foaming out the tops, handed me one, and killed the other. Even though my gut was already beer-heavy, I chugged that Bud like I hadn't had a beer in five years. I bent the can in half, flipped it out the window — never heard it hit the road. Denny opened two more. Then two more. He rocked back and forth to some music that only he could hear. I sagged in my seat, some dizzy, and closed my eyes:

It's the summer me and Denny are ten, and we're bushwhacking through the woods behind the barrel factory. I carry the canteen full of Moxie, Denny guards the Luckies — we don't go nowhere without our smokes. Real eventual, the jungle-green woods thin and there lays a pond. But this ain't some secret swimming hole left over from the days of the granite quarries. I wouldn't have wanted to see what swum in that pond: a festering eye with at least a dozen steel drums half sunk in its still water, which is as thick and black as hot tar fresh-laid on a back road. The pond gives off a bug-spray smell, and the trees that clutch at its bankings have withered to gray. The ground, even the sky, is a puky yellow brown.

We stand there, staring, two kids dumbfounded by a corpse.

Denny shinnies up one of the dead trees. Daring one of the branches, he leans out over the pond, shading his eyes with his hand, and scrutinizes its black surface. He turns and grins at me, and I know that there's a part of him that wants to cannonball into that pond — probably wouldn't even be a splash — just for the hell of it. He screws around, rocks the tree back and forth, back and forth. I want to tell him to stop it, that he's scaring me. But I don't. Don't want him to think I'm a pussy. When you're ten years old, it's better to be dead than be a pussy.

A shudder of knowing — plain out-and-out knowing — passes through me, and I swear I'm running at Denny even before I hear the tree trunk splinter. I imagine Denny sucked into the black water, which oozes oil-like into his mouth and nose. I lower my shoulder and slam full tilt into the falling tree. Denny and the tree fall sideways, squooshing into the muck, not even six inches from the pond.

Me and Denny never talked about it, his almost falling into that pond. It was like a shameful thing between us that meant everything. But we couldn't talk about it, or it would somehow lose its meaning. He never even said thanks. But I understood. I wouldn't have wanted someone to save my life neither.

We hadn't seen any cars since Denny cut the lights miles ago. Like I said, it was late. But when we came up over the rise at the Raymond-Epping line we saw a car coming at us; Denny veered into its lane.

The other driver couldn't see us, a black ghost. We charged closer, the two cars aimed at each other. I kept quiet, sat back, gripped my seat. We closed in. But I didn't sweat. My mouth didn't dry. Fear didn't slink into my gut. Closer. And I'll tell you, I know about fear. Closer. I really do. Denny let off the gas some. Closer. The headlights big, bright. I'm grinding my teeth.

Denny hit the 'vette's lights, laid on the horn. I jumped, smacked my head. Other car jerked to our right. Denny faked that way, cut back, and we swerved clear, left that car sitting there, slantways in the middle of the road, its brake lights burning bright red.

Denny cut the lights again, and all I could hear were the cars shrieking at each other, all I could smell was burning rubber. We kept to the wrong lane, me and my best friend, driving towards sunup.

◢ 8

THE DUROCHERS lived over towards Kingsbrook on Robie's Road, the kind of buckled and broken back road my Grandpa Ora'd called "a piece of string fallen out God's pocket." It didn't go anywheres especially; snaked through Granite some and died. Rust-gnawed trailer houses and gutted tarpaper shacks scabbed the road, which didn't favor many true houses. And it didn't lead to no good fishing nor hunting, wasn't no shortcut to nowheres; but its shoulders were linoleumed with spent rubbers and smashed beer bottles. The Durochers' place stood hulking some ten yards off the road, an old bet against the dark woods. The house's white paint was peeling in great birch bark rolls; tall, angry grasses erupted from the stone foundation; a couple of green shutters hung slantways; the chimneys were shy some bricks; caved-in screen flapped from the front porch; the barn roof sagged: a place meant to be looked at from a passing car. But maybe it was right that a hard-used house hid the Marrying Tree.

The Marrying Tree was a Bible oak, a tree rough with Old Testament bark, so wide that you couldn't get around it and so high you couldn't climb it; a great-grandfather oak that made you want to bloody your knees and shout your sins. It wasn't Sanborn County's only marrying tree, but it was the true one, the old-timers said, with its thousands of branches reaching towards God and its millions of leaves singing His hymns; come winter, they called it Christ's bones. I ain't much of a one for God and all, but I understood. That tree was an argument for something, a damned good one.

Durochers had been getting married in that tree's shadow since anyone could remember anyone remembering. And that's where Stain and Pam Durocher were getting married. Fitting, I guess, given that Denny blamed the tree for Pam's getting pregnant.

"It was one of those warm, misty nights you get in March," Denny'd said, "where the air smells green and makes you all horny. Anyways, I'm bringing her home, and when we get out of the car she drags me out back. Before I know which end is up, we're under that goddamned tree and she's riding me from one end of the county to the other. Swear I shot into her a good two minutes. It was like that tree lit my fuse and set me off forever. And you know what she's saying during all that? 'Marry me, Denny!' she says. 'Marry me!' Jesus H. Christ."

The Marrying Tree wasn't just for Durochers; they were caretakers. Anyone who wanted could get married under that tree, any time; the town charter said so. Some fifty steel folding chairs sat out there year round. Hardly a Graniter lived who hadn't been to at least one wedding out to the Marrying Tree.

I was the first one there. The first to suck in the sweet smell of the wet, fresh-cut grass, the first one to sit — the chair still dewy from the night before — and let the sun that sifted through the Marrying Tree give me what I figured was the closest thing to a blessing that I was ever going to get.

Clutching white flowers, Pam Durocher paused at the top of the grassy aisle between the folding chairs. She stood just shy of the Marrying Tree's shade. The noon sun reflected off her plain white dress (a hint too tight in the belly) and kindled her red hair. The air around her shimmered the way it will out to Route 49 on a hot day. Stain stood alone in the deep shade of the tree, near its trunk. Like me, he had on his best dungarees and a white shirt, except he wore one of those country western string ties held in a silver clasp. I couldn't read Stain's face, though; in the shadows, he was just one more.

"I feel like a piece of shit about this whole thing," I whispered to Dog.

"Don't feel lonesome," he said. "Gives me a gut ache."

Dickie said, "What were we supposed to do?"

"I don't know," I said. "Something."

"Like what?" Dickie said.

"We're Stain's friends," I said. "Friends take care of each other."

At least Denny wasn't there. Stain had invited him, but he hadn't shown. That's all we needed; the way Denny'd been acting he'd have tried to chop down the damned tree.

Pam drifted towards her marriage — the restless leaves the only music — down the aisle, past her grandparents and aunts and uncles and cousins, past her friends. They all seemed on the edge of their seats, wanting to touch her, ready at the least sign to pull her back. But she didn't see them, didn't see any of us. Head held high and defiant — I admired that — she didn't even look at Stain, but up into the Marrying Tree's whispering guts. I wondered what Stain'd gotten himself into.

Mr. Durocher, a short man weighed down by a salami nose, intercepted his daughter, tried to look her in the eye. She wouldn't meet his gaze. A graceless tension between them, he took her small hands in his rough paws, kissed her once on each cheek — a lion pecking at birdseed — and nudged her towards Stain and the church-deep voice of Justice of the Peace Merland Bake. Before moving on, though, Pam did look to her mother, who blushed and smiled shy.

That wedding was as plain as Mrs. Durocher's face, and I was thankful for it. None of that usher-and-bridesmaid bull. No maid of honor, no best man. Just two people getting married — for whatever reasons — and standing before the man doing the job. There was no gussying-up by the friends or relatives: the women wore bright, simple dresses; the men had shaved, pulled on clean pants and a clean shirt, and maybe gambled a splash of Old Spice. Now, *that* was getting dressed up.

Mr. Durocher put on the dog about only one thing: the food. But I guess a man's allowed to be prideful about some small thing.

I got full just looking at all the food laid out at that wedding: mountains of potato, macaroni, and garden salad; slab after slab of ham and roast beef; small sausages and salamis, in-between sausages and salamis, big sausages and salamis; calves' liver swaddled in bacon; vats of shrimp; hard-boiled and pickled eggs; barrels (real wooden barrels from Spalding & Frost's in Fremont) of potato chips, pretzels, and cheese curls; kettles of soup, stew, and chowder; Mason jars of pickles, beets, cauliflower, and broccoli; grilled dogs, burgers, and ribs side by each with baked potatoes and corn on the cob wrapped in tin foil; whole radishes, tomatoes, and cucumbers; a riot of zucchini — food, food, food, everywhere.

Folks woofed it down, too, let me tell you; packed it away fast as it showed. They weren't no amateurs. They'd come to that wedding hungry and they punished that food. I saw more than one person polish off two heaping plates — small hills is more like it — just waiting in line. And they kept coming back, piling it on and shoveling it in. Hands crunched into the chips and pretzels; whole jars of pickles, beets, and broccoli got inhaled; they tore into logjams of salamis and sausages, pyramids of shrimp, and towers of burgers; spoons used like steam shovels leveled those mountains of salad; sandwiches snorted, eggs devoured, the steady *smack, smack, smack* of laboring mouths, an army of eaters set loose. What a feed. I worried over the small kids, though. Figured that if they got too close to the food, they might get picked off.

Then there was the beer. Hundreds, maybe thousands, of bottles and cans: Bud, Schaefer, Black Horse, Schlitz, Genny Cream Ale, Miller, 'Gansett, Black Label, Pickwick, Pabst's Blue Ribbon, Dawson, Ballantine, Old Style, Coors, Fort Schuyler, Rolling Rock, Rheingold, Knickerbocker, and even some scum-topped home brew straight from Mr. Durocher's cellar.

No whiskey, though. "The hard stuff makes alkies," Mr. Durocher said.

After the gorging and the guzzling came the horseshoes. While the women cleaned, or gabbed and gossiped crow-fashion at tables under the Marrying Tree — "Nowadays, most of them are in the family way when they get married" — the men (Stain led by Mr. Durocher) aimed themselves down over the hill, out of sight of the women and the "goddamned kids," to pitch horseshoes on Mr. Durocher's half-dozen horseshoe pits.

"Ever shoot shoes?" Mr. Durocher asked Stain.

"Nope," Stain said.

Mr. Durocher bent over with a grunt — a fat man heaving fastballs — and picked up a horseshoe.

"This is a horseshoe," he said, holding the dusty, U-shaped shoe out to Stain. "See that stake down th'other end? It's forty foot from here. You want to get the shoe round the stake."

Mr. Durocher stood next to the horseshoe pit, crooked his elbow, cocked his arm, swung it back, then forward, letting go of the horseshoe at the top of the swing. The shoe turned one and one half times and landed with a *clink* and a cloud of dust on the far stake — a ringer.

"Here, you try," he said.

Stain held the shoe out straight, swung his arm back, bent his legs, swung his arm forward, and let the shoe go. It arched high in the air, flipping about five times before it whumped down about ten foot short of the pit.

"Try it again," Mr. Durocher said. "This time don't flip it so."

While Mr. Durocher fed Stain horseshoes, more of the men chugged down, some lugging cast-iron tubs of beer on ice. The men shed their shirts just as quick as they'd shed their wives and kids. To the song of steel biting steel and the hiss of poptops and bottle caps, they proceeded to sweat off the wedding.

His shirt off too now, Mr. Durocher sent Stain, Dickie, and Dog off to practice. His wasn't a gentle beer gut, not a petting stomach. Instead, it was a gristly, muscular hump that seemed to shine in the sun. Above that gut, a wave of gray-black hair erupted that smothered his chest and crawled up his neck till it brushed his Adam's apple; looked to me that that hair aimed to strangle him one day, given the chance.

"Beer?" I asked him, holding out a Pabst.

"Thought you'd never ask," he said, his tight face easing some. "Sure's a hot one. Thought that g.d. ceremony'd never get over. Merland Bake sure can go on. So what'd you think?"

"Well . . ." I said. "I ain't been to many weddings."

Mr. Durocher stopped smiling, looked at me direct, a hint of a grin behind his closed lips. "Well, I know what I think," he said. "But I don't talk family with strangers."

He winked, downed his beer in one long swallow. He started working another, but a nagging, bluejay kind of voice ruined his concentration: "Mr. Durocher, can I talk to you?"

Stain's mother, a drought-stricken cornstalk somewhere in her forties, marched up to Mr. D. She was out of place among the men and boys pitching shoes and hammering back beers, and Mr. Durocher's face said, What the hell are you doing here?

"I'm looking for Horace," she said, her voice dry as her skin. "Where is he? I have to go."

"Over there," said Mr. Durocher, jerking his thumb in Stain's direction. "Hope you enjoyed yourself, Mrs. Thistle."

She made a face like she'd just found dog shit smeared on the bottom of her shoe. "I just hope we're satisfied," she said to him. "Know what I mean?"

She heeled away. No thank you's, no friendliness, no nothing. Mr. Durocher looked at me, offered the same knowing wink.

"You shoot shoes?" he asked.

"Some," I said.

"What the hell we waiting on?" he said. "Hey, Red! Get your lard-ass over here. Let's play some partners."

Mr. Durocher killed his beer, wiped his hands on his pants, and picked up four horseshoes. Four snaps of the arm later, the shoes sat on the far stake, piled one atop the other like Sunday morning pancakes.

◢

Frank sat in the dark at the top of the attic stairs, a Schlitz in his left hand and a knife — a broad, flat-bladed job that'd been Bub Duston's — in his right. He'd been sitting there since he'd taken a swipe at Norma. She'd come out to the porch, bitched at him, and he'd turned on her like a dying dog. He'd just missed with the knife, and she'd run out of the house. He hadn't chased her; his point'd been made.

Some instinct had goaded him to retreat to the attic. He couldn't tell how long ago that'd been — an hour? a day? a week? Not that it mattered. Frank savored the dark the way some men fancy a good steak or strong whiskey. To him, the dark was an icy splash in the face with water drawn from a deep, black spring. It cleared his head and, even though fresh sweat smarted his eyes, made him unmindful of the dogged heat. As long as the beer held out, there was no reason to come down. He slouched, snugging his backbone to the edge of the step, shut his eyes, and heard the keening of the Boston & Maine blanket the swamp, blanket everything with the longing and sadness that gnawed at his guts. The train rumbled through his mind — an iron ghost — through the swamp, rolling out of Sanborn County, to the seacoast, where the gulls gossiped at its passing, and then on to Portland and, finally, true north into the heart of the big woods.

Tilting back his head, Frank killed the beer and set the bottle with the other empties that roosted on the step below his feet. But there were plenty of rations left, two sixes in the Styrofoam cooler just begging to be drunk. He gentled the knife to the floor, shaking as he reached for another beer, which he cracked with a hiss of the wrist. Choking the bottle with both hands, he chugged the cold beer so it burned his throat. He belched, wiped his mouth with an arm. To stop the shakes, which had come again, he gripped the knife so it hurt his hands and tried to conjure up that B & M freight that would bear him away, save him.

Earl would like the logging camps. Strong boy. Good boy. Should get away from all this shit. Me and him should just screw everything, like he said. Jump that B & M. Teach him to live like a man. Sat'day night we'd head into town, get crocked, hunt up somethin' strange. One hell of a time.

Frank snapped open another brew. Took a gulp. Half held, half balanced the bottle on his bare, hard stomach. The bottle's cold sweat soothed him.

Got to get. Get free. Hop on that ol' freight. No more putting up with no one's shit. No more busting balls. No more cunt trouble. Women. Can't depend on 'em. Go whore-ish, give 'em half a chance. Cunts. Ungrateful. Wished I hadn't a missed. Buried that knife in her heart. Would've showed her.

He downed the beer but held the empty, picking at the label, peeling it, letting the attic dark break over him.

"Hey, Frank, you miserable sonuvabitch! What t'hell you doing up there?"

Frank bolted up, rousted from his dream.

"Y'going to answer me, Frank?"

Frank loosened some. Only Leon. Norma'd run to Leon like she always did — the caller of the semiregular square dances between the two men.

"Pound sand, Leon," Frank said. "Go fuck yourself."

Leon George stood at the bottom of the stairs, the attic door closed behind him, peering up into the darkness. Frank stared down. They couldn't see each other, only a hint of edgy shadows rustling in the dark.

"Look, you old cocksucker," Leon reasoned. "I didn't come all the way out here to listen to your shit. You coming down? Or do I have to come up there and drag you down by the balls?"

"Try it."

Leon took out his handkerchief, sopped up the sweat on his face. A stalling tic, really — a pitcher kneading the rosin bag after he's just walked the bases loaded — as he tried to decipher that afternoon's make of Frank Sargent. He'd arrested them all, from the snake-silent predator to the sobbing drunk. Somewhere in the rubble lay a man Leon liked and respected.

"I'm pissed, Frank. Sunday's my day off. There I was, watching the Sox on TV, a six in the icebox, and then I have to come all the way out here and haul your ass out the attic — again."

Leon paused. "I could've called in the staties, you know. Then you really would've been up shit's creek."

"Bullshit!" roared Frank, who knew that Leon George took care of his own. 'Course, that didn't keep Frank from winging an empty at him.

"Sounded low and outside," Leon said as he stepped onto the stairs.

"Stay back, you bastard," Frank said. "I'll cut you like a pig."

"Frank, if I was worried 'bout that, I'd shoot your ass where you sit. How many times we going to do this? Last time it was an ax, time before a shotgun. When you going to smarten up?"

"You tell that moldy bitch of mine to smarten up."

"Frank, there ain't nothin' I can do about that. Wish there was, but there ain't."

Frank's granite-hard hate melted some, softened into a thing that made his gut churn, made him disgusted with himself. He couldn't help it, but he was whining. "Wished I hadn't a missed, Leon. Wished I'd a slit her up real good.

"I'm getting old, Leon. Old. And the boy — Earl — the boy needs a man around.

"Don't know why in hell I'm up here. This is my house, ain't it? Built it myself. I don't have to hide in it like a crook or something. Know where I wished I was? Wish I was in one of those logging camps down to Maine. Grew up logging. Ever tell you that?"

Frank didn't move when Leon took the knife from him.

"It'd be good for Earl to work the woods, Leon. Don't you think?"

Leon stood on the step in front of Frank and shook his head. The county wouldn't be letting Frank out after only a couple of weeks this time; Frank needed to take the cure. What was it happened to Frank Sargent? What made him hurt so? Leon didn't pity him, though. Leon never pitied anyone. You either helped a body in trouble, he figured, or ignored him; pity was salt in a wound.

Frank grabbed a beer.

"Another one?" Leon asked.

"What t'hell's the difference? Going to be my last one for a while, ain't it?"

Leon nodded. "Ain't too much beer over to the County Farm."

Frank started down the stairs, one hand fingertipping the wall, as halting as a two-year-old. Leon hefted the knife, weighed it as if it might tell him something about Frank. He shrugged, thunked it into the top step, and followed Frank down the stairs, through the house, and outdoors.

Norma sat in Leon's air-conditioned cruiser and stared at the two men as they sat on the front steps and talked, Frank squinting in the bright sun.

She realized that she was somewhat let down that at least one of them wasn't bleeding.

◢

It had grown dusky. The sun had dropped behind the trees, but its raw, red scars seeped through the woods; soon, the mosquitoes would be unbearable for most folks. But we still drank, shot shoes. Hardly anyone had left the wedding. We were caught up in it — shouting, laughing, swearing, giving each other general shit. A few hours like that, bending steel to our needs, made up for a lot. Once in a while, a wife or a little kid stood on top of the hill above the pits. Arms folded, the wife would tap her foot and glare down at the husband, who always smiled back, taking a swig of beer, and kept on playing. The kids asked, "Daddy, when we going home?" And the father'd snap, "When I'm goddamned good and ready." The kid'd scoot back to Mommy with the news.

Me and Dickie — dusty, dirty, and sweaty — sat on the bench doing home brew. The beer, though it wasn't much more than glorified skunk piss, soothed us.

"What a day, huh?" Dickie said.

"Been good," I said. "Pam's old man's all right."

We sucked on our beers, watched Stain and Mr. Durocher play two of his brothers, who carried Firestone guts and side-of-beef arms, too. Stain, horseshoe-stake skinny, looked like a snack for the brothers Durocher. Stain tossed his shoe; it bounced and bounded past the pit, Mr. Durocher doing a jig to avoid getting shinned.

"Hey! Take the horse off that shoe!" he shouted.

Stain threw again and the shoe slid into the pit, a runner stealing second, and looped around the stake for a ringer. "Attaboy, Stain!" Mr. Durocher yelled. "Keep that up, you'll be part of this family yet."

Grinning drunk, Stain's jaw sagged and his teeth showed. Hadn't seen his new wife all afternoon. But what the fuck, his father-in-law was taking care of him, right?

"Stain and the old man're sure hitting it off," Dickie said.

"Well," I said, "Stain ain't got no father, and the old man's got six daughters. You figure it out."

"Good match."

"Better'n Stain and Pam."

"Yeah."

"I bet it'll be one of those things where Stain'll be friends with the old man even after Stain and Pam split up."

Dickie looked at me — "Ain't you the fucking optimist?" — and I shrugged.

"Hey, you want to find another partner?" I said. "I got to take a piss somethin' fierce."

I trudged up the hill towards the house, breathing in that certain damp that belongs to dusk. Behind me, the horseshoes talked, punctuating the dying day. The women still sat under the Marrying Tree — children asleep on their laps — their voices low, ripe with meaning, sometimes a giggle flaring, fading. They looked up as I crested the hill, then looked away. I wasn't one of theirs.

On the back porch, two porky kids were parked at a strawberry-rhubarb pie. I asked them for the bathroom. "Top the stairs," said the bigger one, showing off a mouthful of pie.

"Thanks," I said. "Don't eat too much pie, now." They grinned sticky, strawberry-rhubarb grins.

The house drowsed still and shadowy, stuffy after the

day's heat, and slinking through its twilight made me feel drunker: rooms swayed, furniture rustled. Grabbing the railing, I walked upstairs, which gave off a musty, old-house smell that I liked — an overstuffed chair left down cellar too long. Made me think of the house that me, Ma, and Bub'd lived in till I was five.

In the bathroom, I realized that the Durochers' truly was a house of women and girls: soggy stockings and pantyhose hung from the shower rod, cardboard boxes of tampons and panty shields sat stacked in the corners. On the shelves stood five different kinds of cock-shaped deodorant, eleven brands of shampoo, an army of perfumes, clouds of sterile cotton, a rainbow of lipsticks, jar upon jar of lotions, creams, make-up, and peroxide, boxes of Q-tips, and six each of Johnson's Baby Oil and Johnson's Baby Powder, which made the room smell like a baby's butt. No wonder Mr. Durocher had built six horseshoe pits.

Sitting on the toilet, I hunched forward, holding my face in my hands, trying to stop the dizziness. It worked some, and my head settled. It's always strange to use someone else's bathroom — Ma never would; she'd piss her pants first — because that's where you can tell character. It's easy enough to straighten up the living room before company comes, but the bathroom — that's where the secrets, slimy with mold and mildew, live. Families don't hide their skeletons in closets no more; they ditch them in the bathroom.

Out in the darkening hall, I leaned against the wall, leaving a sweat mark. I heard the horseshoes and the women, but they seemed far away — ghost sounds.

I thought I heard Denny.

No words, but his low growl. I bent my head forward, concentrating, like listening for a mosquito. I heard it again.

I staggered soft down the hall, saw a door that was open a

crack, and looked in. In the grainy half light Denny and Pam stood close, closer than Stain and Pam had at the wedding, the hiss of their whispers coiling and uncoiling. I kneeled, watched. Don't know why I didn't stop it right there. Maybe that miserable sonuvabitch that's in me decided Stain deserved this, that somebody had to witness his shame.

Pam rubbed against Denny the way a cat in heat will take to your ankle. Her hands slithered down his pants. She undid them, let them pool at his ankles, and buried her hands and face in his crotch. He hiked her wedding dress up around her waist — she didn't have underpants on — and hefted her at an angle, his back bowed, and slid into her. The folds of her dress draped them as she rose up and down, hoisted in the air, riding Denny like some merry-go-round.

I turned away, my gut churning like it was a work day. I'd seen enough, too much. In the watching, in the knowing, I felt like I'd fucked Pam Durocher — Pam Thistle — just as sure as Denny. I lurched down the hall, feeling emptier and darker than I had in a long time. Denny may as well have taken a knife and gutted me.

◢ 9

MIDNIGHT closed in — all the lights still on in the Durochers' house, shadows guttering at the windows — and me and Stain sat next to each other, slouched against the Marrying Tree. Felt good to lean on something solid; I needed that right then.

"Man, am I loaded," Stain said. "Don't think I've ever been this drunk."

"Been some day," I said.

"Can't fucking believe I'm really married."

"Me neither."

"You ever getting married?"

"I guess. Used to think me and Mary was going to get married. But that was kid shit, you know? Ain't in no rush."

"Tell you one thing, Earl."

"What's that?"

"I know for a God-honest fact that Kate Mallory's just itching for you."

"Kate Mallory? What kind of bull you trying to feed me?"

"Ain't shitting you, Earl. Got my sources; I hear things over to the garage."

"Kate's a good kid."

"Check it out, Earl."

Stain tore open a piece of Juicy Fruit; the gum wrapper's crinkling sounded unnatural loud in the dark.

"Gum?" Stain asked.

"No thanks," I said. "Trying to quit."

We laughed.

"Did I tell you I got a new car?" Stain asked. "Picked it up couple days ago. 'Sixty-seven Dart. Slant six. No rust. Traded that 'sixty-five Ponny even up."

"Sounds good," I said.

"Got it for the honeymoon. We're gonna drive up Wolfeboro tomorrow. Pam's folks got a summer camp up there on the lake. Staying a week."

"Surprised that sonuvabitch you work for give you the week."

"Aw, Vernon ain't that bad. He lets me work on my own cars in the garage and stuff. Plus he gives me some off on parts."

"Gonna stay there a while?"

"Well, Vernon says he's going to make me number one man when old Dean retires. Shouldn't be too long now."

"Sounds pretty good."

"Yut, yut. It's steady."

"Pam going to keep working at Bolton's?"

"Till the baby anyways."

The baby. Those two words sure stopped us cold. We'd forgot all about the baby. The goddamned baby. Ain't got no baby, you ain't got no wedding.

"What do you think about all that?" I asked. "The baby and stuff."

"Oh, it'll work out," Stain said.

"You got a lot of balls, man. Don't know what I'd do if I got some girl pregnant."

Stain looked at me in a way he never had before. I can't put my finger on it exact. The best I can say is that he looked at me the way a man would — not some kid.

"You don't have to pretend for my sake," he said, sounding a little ticked off. "I ain't stupid, you know. I know that baby ain't mine. I know it's Denny fucking Gamble's. But I don't care. Maybe me and Pam don't love each other or nothing, but we got an understanding — and maybe that's even better. I give the baby a name — and, believe me, there's worse than Thistle — and she treats me like a husband and I treat her like a wife. I don't think that's so bad. I'm a hard worker. We'll do all right.

"And she's beautiful, Earl. So goddamned beautiful. I couldn't've ever gotten a girl that good-looking without some finagling. It's what I do best, you know.

"Look at me, Earl. I'm one ugly bastard, ain't I? Got that big purple birthmark smeared all over my face. So who was I supposed to end up with? Marilyn Dickens? Connie Saint Clair? They're both homelier'n a cartload of assholes. You fucking guys were probably saving up all your flags for me. 'That's it, Stain. Drape a flag over her face and fuck her for Old Glory!' Screw that shit.

"Tell you one thing, Pam don't call me Stain. She calls me Horace or she don't call me nothing.

"Nope, I really don't care what nobody thinks. I'm one lucky sonuvabitch, putting it to a girl like Pam Durocher. I'd be the first one to admit it. Don't know what in hell Gamble's problem was. But I ain't bitching. His loss is my gain. What a frigging asshole that guy is, and I don't care if you are his friend. She says she still loves him, you know. But I don't believe her. Don't give a shit, either. I got something of Denny Gamble's and I ain't giving it back till I'm good and ready. I got that prick by his short hairs.

"But you know what the best part is, Earl? This'll make getting the next one that much easier. I ain't fooling myself or nothing. I know this thing with Pam ain't gonna last forever. I'm just gonna get my pecker's worth and see what happens. But you get that first pretty one and you got it dicked. All the other ones think you must really have something on the ball, and they can't wait to check it out. And I'm going to be ready.

"Tell you another thing, Earl. In ten years I'm going to be married to a woman even prettier than Pam Durocher and I'm gonna be driving me a brand-new Caddy and I'm gonna own Vernon's garage. I'll tell you that right now."

Stain. Always trading up.

◢

Ma was passed out in her rocking chair, mouth ajar, B & M breathing. It surprised me to see her. When I came in that late the house generally belonged to me — dark, Frank and Ma asleep. I'd sobered up pretty good from the wedding — wasn't even that tired — and I'd planned on taking to the porch to think on Denny and Stain till their troubles put me to sleep. Given the chance, though, I studied Ma's face: ragged ditches stitched her forehead instead of the gentle lines of middle age. Deep ditches, I knew; I'd lived through most the digging.

Whenever I saw her sitting in that rocker, I'd remember a time some months after Bub had walked out on us. We lived in a two-room shack, slapped on a concrete slab, over to Kelley Road then. Just the two of us, on the relief. I'd spent the day shoveling chicken shit at Bennett's Egg Farm for a buck-fifty an hour. When I come home, Ma's coiled in that rocker, swilling hard stuff — she's been drinking worse and worser since Bub — and her eyes shine blank and hollow.

"Hi, Ma," I says. "Hot one today."

She doesn't say nothin', squints at me with those snapping-turtle eyes of hers. "Where you been all day?" she asks finally. "Been looking for you."

"I told you this morning I was going to be working at Bennett's."

"Bennett's."

"Been there all day."

"I've been wanting you to walk over to Frankie Foss's store and pick up a few things."

"Okay. But I got to go to the bathroom first."

"I want to get supper started, Earl."

"Okay. But I gotta go."

I walk towards the closet-sized room where we keep the slop pail; we don't even have an outhouse. Ma looks at me cockeyed, like she don't understand what I'm doing.

"Earl," she says, rocking. "I want you to go to Frankie Foss's. Now."

"Jesus, Ma," I says. "Want me to shit my pants?"

"Don't you talk to me like that, Earl Duston."

She beets up, takes another chorus on the bottle, and rocks faster. The floorboards groan.

"Just 'cause you're bigger'n me," she says, "don't mean you can get too big for your britches."

I shrug, walk into the bathroom, shut the door, and plant myself on the enamel pail. My back is stiff against the wall and the soles of my shoes are flush to the door. To make matters worse, a fly strip the color of old Scotch tape hangs about halfway down the ceiling so that when you're sitting on the can some twenty crunchy dead flies dance right in front of your nose. At least a breeze is blowing through the open window — and I'm not in the same room with Ma.

She rocks harder, faster — the chair screeking, bitching.

"Goddamn you," she says. "I told you to go to the store."

I say nothing and suck in the lukewarm breeze. The rocking ceases. I picture Ma stopping the chair once she stands up; she can't abide an empty rocker's rocking—means someone's about to die, she says. During thunder showers she hides under the bed; says the thunder is God cleaning house and that we aren't supposed to see it.

"I'm hungry!" she shouts. "Ain't had a damned thing to eat all day. You better have your ass out here by the time I count to five or I'll come in and drag you out. One!"

Sighing, I latch the door, look out the window, which faces the frog pond down the hill.

"Two!"

I hear her walking, but away from me.

"Three!"

She rattles in the silverware drawer. The edge to her voice makes me wince. It's a voice that drips fear, frustration, and hate. She ain't strong enough, and she doesn't have nobody 'cept me. And I look too much like Bub, she says.

"Four! Goddammit, Earl, get your ass out here!"

I don't know what to do no more.

"Five! You little bastard!" she shrieks. "I'll fix you!"

Sounds like she's on fire, her voice crackling, almost crazy. I'm done, but I'm sure as hell not going out there till she quiets. I look to the green, scum-covered pond; the frogs start to peep and croak.

"You coming out?" she hollers.

Glass shatters against the door, makes me jump; I almost knock over the slop pail. She tries the door, and I hear her breathing. The way she heaves, you'd think she's run to Frankie Foss's and back.

"Huh?" she shouts. "Huh?"

"Ma," I say.

Wood splinters every which way and the door cracks in two as the broad, big-handled knife bulls through. Ma hauls off, hacks again, and the door pops open. She sways in front of me, a sad, skinny ghost swaddled in the shack's dusk, two-handing the knife with its thick oak handle and wide, sharp blade; Bub's old knife. She hefts it, lunges at the door once more, even though it's open. Before she can move again, I'm out the window.

"I'll get you, Bub," she spits. "I'll get you and chop off your prick of misery."

I run around the shack onto Kelley Road. Ma hurries out the front door. But I'm gone, way up the road. I stop, look down the hill at her. She almost looks comical, apron on, scampering, holding the knife above her head. I turn away — I still have the money from Bennett's — and lope up the road in the half light.

Ma shouts, "I'll get you, Bub, you bastard! I'll get you!"

Her voice sounds like I'm hearing it late at night on the radio, some faraway station that you can hardly hear for the static and whistling. The knife clangs on the road.

I spend the night at Denny's; I don't go home for three days.

We had quite the times, all right, after Bub lit out. Hell, they were probably worse before he left. But at least we ate regular in between the beatings.

I was tempted to let Ma sleep in the rocker, but I knew it'd raise hell with her back. I wondered where Frank was; probably out to the porch, sleeping one off. I gentled Ma's shoulders. She thrashed some, made those drowning noises people make when they're waking up, then considered me with her bloodshot eyes.

"Lea' me 'lone," she said. "Sleep."

"Ma," I said. "Your back."

"Lea' me 'lone."

She closed her eyes. I touched her shoulders again.

"Ma? Ma? You okay? You been crying?"

No answer.

"Ma?"

"Never mind," she said, more awake now, pissed off. "Ain't none of your damned business."

"What's the matter?" I asked, trying hard to be patient.

"Leave me alone," she said, her voice raw as a skun knee.

"What's wrong?"

"For Christ's sakes, will you leave me alone? You're worse than a little old lady." She paused, catching her breath. "Leon came and took Frank away to the County Farm. All right? You happy now? Bastard tried to kill me."

So he'd gone and done it again, tried to shut Ma up permanent. Frank. When the guy was sober he'd give you the shirt off his back. Get him drunk . . .

"Why do you stay with him, Ma?"

When she finally answered, she spoke soft and weary, wouldn't look at me. "Woman needs a man, Earl. In this world, anyways. Don't matter what kind of no-good sonuvabitch he is long as he'll stay. And I don't care what else Frank is, but he's a stayer. I know that. I've given him rope enough to leave. Uh-huh, Frank's a stayer. He'd kill me before he'd leave me. That's right. He only swings that ax at me or scares me with the shotgun because he loves me. That's why he hits me, too. Wants me to be a good girl. His girl."

Ma stumbled, crying now.

"We're all made to be run out on," she said. "Women, I mean. You know, broads, dames, sluts, whores. Cunt. We're good at getting left behind, thrown over like an old piece of furniture alongside the road. My father left me first; that was after my mother passed away. Next was the boy got me in the family way at the foster home. That was a good one there. That boy, my foster parents' son, run away. He was seventeen, eighteen. When his folks figured out what'd happened, they sent me away, back to the orphanage up to Franklin. I was fourteen, and I had the baby at the orphanage. A girl. I run away, left her there.

"Then Bub. Men before him. Men after him. Made for desertion, we are. Bub surprised me, though. Not that he left, but how he left. Didn't think he was a coward. He was a hard man, your father. Had a face all bones and angles, like yours; always thought I'd cut myself on it when I touched it. I would a rather stroked a razor blade than his face sometimes.

"But I don't get surprised no more. Someday Frank'll leave me, I guess. I'm kind of like an old circus — they have small circuses like that anymore, like the ones that used to come round the orphanage? — that goes from town to town, getting seedier and seedier, more rundown every trip. At each town, the stops get shorter and shorter. Finally, you have to fold up your tents for good, be all alone. Me and that circus, same difference.

"Frank'll go. The others. You. Don't blame you, I guess. I ain't much of a mother."

"Huh?"

"You'll desert me, too. It's a man's nature."

"I'm your son."

"So?"

"I ain't one of your damned boyfriends. I don't owe you nothin'."

"You'll see, Earl. Everyone leaves me."

My face flushed, my fists doubled. I wanted to yell at her,

level her with my voice. I gritted my teeth till my jaw hurt. I hated her right then. Hated her as much as I hated Bub. Maybe more. Bub might've beat me and walked out on us, but she was the one put up with his shit, hoping he'd stay. She was the one let Bub hit me, let him walk. Bet she knew exactly where Bub was headed that winter morning. She was the one who was so goddamned stupid, who kept finding guys just like Bub. Guys who'd drink with her, fuck her, then beat her. Whether it was Bub, Frank, or some other prick, that's what she wanted: a cock shoved between her legs, a bottle to her mouth, and a fist in her face. It fit her ideas.

"You miserable old cunt."

She turned, looked up at me. "When you were born," she said, sharpening each word, "I kept hoping one of us would die. Never did get over that feeling."

I retreated to my room and, there in the dark, burrowed beyond sleep, into the past:

I'm seven years old. It's early December, cold, and me and Bub wait in the car outside Dr. Lee's office in Lamprey; Ma's inside. I sit in the back seat, coloring stock cars and dragsters with my Crayola eight-pack. Bub sits quiet in front, his back to me, smoking and staring out the window. I can see my breath when I blow and my feet are starting to hurt.

It's ten miles from our place to Dr. Lee's, and I always take in those ten miles of road like they're a different country.

The Lamprey Road doesn't pick up steam till those right-left-right, roller-coaster turns just before the Piscataway Campground. The turns where Young Joe Gaudet flipped over his Mustang and got paralyzed; Young Joe dressed out at a good three hundred pounds then, and it took the fire department the better part of five hours to cut him out of the car. Anyways, Bub slams through those turns like nothing, the Chevy's tires squealing. It don't bother me, but Ma's already gripping the dashboard, her feet stomping brakes that ain't there. She looks at Bub, means to say something, but doesn't. She turns away, looks out the window.

We pass the Agway, where Bub buys feed for his gamecocks, drop into a dip that flip-flops my stomach, and barrel through a sweeping curve that straightens past Stevens' farm, where they grow the best sweet corn in all Granite. Bub's almost smiling as the houses, barns, and fields flicker by.

After the pick-your-own berries stand, Bub tromps on the gas as we gallop up the short side of Great Hill.

"Hold on, Earl," Bub says. "Here it comes."

Great Hill's so steep that on the way down it seems you can't help but bury your car's nose in the pavement. Not only that, it flattens out into a left-hand curve that switches quick to the right, then funnels into a 45-degree left-hander that shoots you down another hill, over a skinny bridge, and on into Lamprey. It's usually at the top of Great Hill that Ma shuts her eyes and slinks low in her seat. But Bub has it down; if nothing else, the bastard can drive.

Bub floors it — the engine vibrates through the soles of my feet — so it seems we're going to smack head on into the trees that stand at the bottom of Great Hill. But Bub jams the brakes, downshifts, and we slide through the curve, tires screaming this time, car straining to roll over. Manhandling the steering wheel, Bub gets us through the right turn, the next left, and before I know it, we're cranking by the Lamprey Brickyard. Dr. Lee's is only a half mile more.

*

Ma's crying as she steps careful out of the doctor's office.

Bub, when he sees her, growls, "Shit."

She gets in the car, but I don't look up, pretend to color.

"Well?" Bub says.

Ma's just about killed her tears; we both know better than to cry in front of Bub. "If you want to cry, I'll give you something to cry about" is what he always says. Ma blows her nose.

"Well, goddammit?" Bub says.

Ma doesn't say nothing. I peek up; she's staring at her lap.

"This is all we fucking need," Bub says. "This is just wonderful. We ain't got enough goddamned worries."

My face prickles with the knowing that something important has happened. But I can't figure it out. I wrinkle my forehead, listen harder.

"You're really some kind of bitch, ain't you, Norma? Just some kind of fucking, sneaky bitch."

Ma looks at me, then at Bub. "Little ears," she says.

Bub lays rubber as we pull out, and I smell burning tires the whole ride home.

That night, after I'm in bed and have almost escaped into sleep, they start arguing in the kitchen. Can't hear the words, just feel their hatefulness quiver in my gut. Bub is fierce thunder that shakes the house, and Ma is a begging whine that pains my ears. I slither under the covers to where it's dark and animal-warm, shut my eyes, and stick my fingers in my ears. I feel like I might throw up as the hot tears come.

It's early morning a few days later. Night has given way to a low, gray sky; smells like snow. Bird Choate's already picked Bub up for work — they're logging all the way over to Fremont and won't be back till late — and I help Ma carry blankets to the car. We must have five or six stacked on the back seat. Ma's already started the car, so when we get in it's warm. I stick my face in front of the heater, which is on full blast, and let the hot air tingle my cheeks and dance my hair.

"Earl, cut it out," Ma snaps, and I slump back into the seat.

"Ma?" I ask. "Where we going?"

"For a ride," she says.

"Yeah, but where?"

"What're you, writing a book or somethin'?"

We pull into the Jenny station — a full green wreath hangs on its door — and Ma asks Ray Dufour to fill it.

"Long trip?" Ray asks, good-natured.

Ma doesn't answer and Ray shrugs. I ain't never seen neither of my folks fill the car before. Only rich people do that. Ma and Bub usually buy their gasoline a buck or two at a whack.

Five minutes later, we're sneaking down the Lake Road, Ma easing over the frost heaves and through the ruts. She drives hunched over the steering wheel, eagle-eyeing the road. She hasn't said a word since we left the gas station. She's settled her mind on something, I know. I can tell from the set to her face: jaw firm, eyes squinted. It's a look I seen on her face the time she poured all Bub's beer down the sink, the time she slapped Bub's face so hard she left a hand-shaped red mark.

Ma hits the brakes, backs up, and turns left down a dirt road that's barely wide enough. The December trees' skeleton branches grab at the Chevy, lashing it as we lurch ahead. I almost smack my head on the dashboard a couple times.

We creep out the woods and onto a small beach on Granite Lake, a beach nobody knows about. Ma stops the car, setting the emergency brake, but leaves it running.

The lake is choppy and padlock-gray — winter water. Ma, chewing her bottom lip, leans back, stares. She slides a small, smooth stone from her breast pocket, slips it into her mouth, and sucks on it. It's her lucky piece of granite; she's had it since she was a girl up to Franklin. She takes comfort from it the way a baby does from its thumb.

"Earl," Ma says as she reaches around and spreads a couple of blankets on the back seat. "Your ma has got to go for a swim. And I want you to stay in this car no matter what. You think it's going to stall, you just push on that gas pedal till it sounds good."

"Okay, Ma," I say.

She moves towards me like she's going to kiss me or something, but at the last second she ducks away. Her hand brushes my cheek.

When you're a little kid, things happen to you and around you that you can't understand. I know it ain't good to swim Granite Lake in December, but Ma knows what she's doing, right? It isn't till I grow up that I figure it out.

Ma gets out of the car and strips. I've never seen her naked before. My ears and cheeks burn, and there's a stirring like small animals in my crotch — but I don't look away. Her nipples, like toy soldiers, stand stiff in the cold, and there's the slight rounding of her belly, which slopes into all that black curly hair. And right then I want my ma back in that car. I want her to hug me, let me rest my cheek on her chest. But she doesn't even look at me.

As she stands there, studying the water and rubbing her arms against the cold, I know of a sudden that Bub has something to do with this, know that Ma wouldn't be testing the cruel water if it wasn't for him. And, for a second, it seems Bub might be right there in that car with me. I shiver.

Ma wades into the lake and when the water's deep enough, pushes off and swims. But I ain't scared for her. Ma's tough. I rest my chin on the dust-smelling dashboard for I don't know how long, my ear grazing the grimy plastic Jesus, and watch Ma make her peace with Granite Lake.

Lips blue, skin potato-pale, Ma crawls into the warm car and collapses onto the back seat. I pull the blankets tight around her.

She looks up at me, the most helpless I've ever seen her, puts out her arms, and I snuggle in next to her. And, like I've always wanted and imagined, she pulls me to her, holds me like she thinks I can save her life. But the only reason she does it, I understand, is because I'm warm and she's death-cold.

10

AT QUARTER TO FOUR — imagining I was gouging Johnson's eyes out — I jammed the track's red off button, slumped onto my milk crate, and whung my gloves at Barnaby, who'd already shut the blaster; he'd flipped a drum on its side and sat on it, keeping down the dust in his lungs with a Marlboro. I closed my eyes and leaned my head back against the wall. Drum factory sure whupped a body — and the day'd gone pretty good. On bad days, I'd had paint guns blow up in my face, falling drums split my head open, acid slop into my boots, rats jump out of the toilet at me. And that wasn't the half of it.

Sometimes I felt like a sorry character in some country song, some Hank Williams moaner about a guy who's been hard-used. The best country music did make me feel the song was about me, my life. Ain't talking about that fancy shit with all the strings and such. I'm talking simple music sung by people who don't sing that good but have stories to tell. To me, the perfect country singer is a guy sitting alone in a dim-lit bar, wearing dungarees and a flannel shirt, playing a plain old guitar and singing stories.

Dirty Willy killed the cover blaster, which coughed as it give up for the day. Willy started stacking covers next to his machine, getting ready for the next morning. Good man, that Dirty Willy.

Homer and Lurch, who worked out back, drifted towards Barnaby, Lurch lugging his big black workingman's lunchbox. Damned thing could've held a tire jack and a spare and still had room for a couple of sandwiches.

Other machines whined down. Drums didn't clang heavy and hollow as the factory quietened and got about as still as it could. The electric still hummed; water dripped — *plop-drop, plop-drop* — into scabby pools; and the compressor, which fed air to the machines, chugged and chuffed. Dust and steam still hung in the air, but not as thick. It seemed the place had been bombed about half an hour before, instead of half a minute. Barnaby kindled another smoke, and Lurch, Homer, and him laughed about something. Their laughing made me smile for a second.

Dickie, bent about double, walked in through the doorway. Almost four o'clock.

"What a day, huh?" Dickie said.

"Yeah," I said. "Like to sweat my balls off."

Of a sudden, Dickie fixed his eyes over my shoulder. I didn't need to look to know that Johnson stood behind me, cheeks reddening, hands on his hips — the predictable prick.

"Duston," Johnson said, "I ought to can your ass. It ain't four yet."

Johnson wore his rat smirk, the one that showed his rotting teeth to best advantage.

"Johnson," I said, "why don't you go shove it up Old Man Fecteau's bunghole."

About to answer me back — the two of us could go on a

good ten minutes like that — he saw that Dirty Willy'd stopped stacking covers. Sensing easier prey, and seeing that everyone was looking at him, Johnson turned on Willy. "What do you think this is, Willy? The relief? We ain't paying you to stand around with your fingers up your ass. You fucking well work until that buzzer goes off. Understand me? You don't, you'll find your filthy ass out the door. You'll get to hug your goddamned chickens all day long because you won't have to come here no more. No one screws the dog on me. Nobody."

Willy's lips trembled, his jaw working hard, but the words wouldn't come. He sounded like a car that won't start of a cold winter's morning. Willy blinked, sputtered, and flinched at Johnson's ranting; Johnson may as well have taken a pickax to him. Willy could protect himself in a fistfight, but he was helpless in a shouting match, a boxer run too ragged to hold up his arms to block the punches. Willy looked at us — me, Dickie, Barnaby, Homer, Lurch — but we stared at the floor, at the ceiling, out the window, anywheres but at him. I'm sorry, but Dirty Willy wasn't worth putting your ass on the line.

"F-f-fuck you guys," he spit out. "P-pussies." He turned his back on us, slunk away. Johnson grinned, whistled "Whistle While You Work" as he strutted off.

Finally, some five minutes late, the buzzer blatted.

Our boots thudded on the cement, some fifty guys racing towards the time clock. The lunchroom door banged open and we poured through, a big grubby mess of men. We rushed down the stairs — me and Dickie wedged midpack — then jockeyed for position at the clock, blocking out like we were trying to pull down a rebound in basketball; I never was much one for basketball, but let me tell you I was one hellacious rebounder. Elbows flew, time cards fell, rumps butted, hands shoved, shoulders lowered and rammed like it mattered who got out first. As if to stay any longer than you had to meant you could never leave.

"Fuck's the holdup?" complained Braley, leaning on me and reaching over to snag his card. "Fuck's the holdup?"

I elbowed him one in the gut, knocking the air out of him. He glared at me but got off my back.

Amid the shouting, swearing, and flailing bodies, Bill and Ray sat at one of the lunch tables and drank their ice tea, Bill still wearing his hard hat. "Got as many kids as I got," Bill told me once, "and I bet you wouldn't be in no hurry to get home."

Andy hadn't rushed, either. He'd take a leak, smoke a butt, talk with Bill and Ray. Then, finally, he'd punch out, amble out the door, ease into his car, and crawl up the hill onto the highway. It was like, in his slowness, he was showing the factory that he could take it, that he wasn't so beat up that he had to run away from the bully as fast as he could. It seemed the harder Andy'd been worked on a given day, the longer it took him to go home.

Me and Dickie let the door slam behind us — I squinted, sucked in the air, which almost smelled good — and headed for his monster, a '68 Buick that Stain'd raised from the dead. I opened the door and got in. Dick had to crawl in through the open window on the driver's side because his door was roped shut. The car stank of stale beer and one of those pine tree-shaped air fresheners that give off a baby powder smell; it dangled from the cigarette lighter, which didn't work. Dead cigarette lighter or not, the ashtray still overflowed with cigarettes, some smeared with pink lipstick, in addition to matches, gum, bottle caps, and spent rubbers. The floor was ankle-deep in beer and tonic bottles, burger wrappers, sand, and more dead butts. I remembered right then why I didn't ride with Dickie much.

He pumped the gas a couple times, turned the key, and the Buick rumbled to life for a few seconds, shuddering my backbone before it cut out.

"Come on, bitch," Dickie coaxed.

They were really hauling ass from the factory now. Rusty threw open the door of his royal blue Road Runner, jumped in, fired it up, spun his wheels in the gravel, and bolted, trailing a cloud of dust. Lurch peeled out in his Jeep, spattering wads of sand onto Johnson's new Caddy; he wrenched the gears furious as he sped up the hill, the Jeep's ass end fishtailing. Marcel in his pickup and G.I. Joe in his Dart raced towards Route 49. Marcel slashed straight ahead, G.I. trying to skirt around him. At the top of the hill, Marcel cut him off and gave him the finger. G.I. nudged Marcel's truck, and they squealed onto the road.

Watching those guys barrel-ass towards home, you'd have thought they took serious what it said on their license plates — what it said on all New Hampshire license plates: "Live Free or Die." That always struck me as a hell of a thing to put on a license plate — not that I didn't believe in it. Somehow it seemed to be an invite to speed; you can't live free or die if you can't go more'n fifty-five miles an hour. I imagined all those cars getting racked up on Route 49 as they were in the process of living free or dying. 'Course, it was a big improvement over what the plates'd said when I was a kid: "Scenic." Sounded like we were the Pansy State, instead of the Granite State. At least "Live Free or Die" had some stones to it.

Dickie pumped the gas again, turned the key. The Buick jerked to life, Dick pumping the gas something fierce as the car shook, quivered, and sputtered, kind of like Dirty Willy.

Finally, a huge gassy roar burst from the engine. Dickie took his foot off the gas and let her idle rough for a few seconds.

"Temperamental, huh?" I said.

"Yeah," Dickie said, shoving it into drive. "That god-damned Stain. I gotta get rid of this piece of shit. I might buy Rusty's Road Runner. He needs some cash."

The Buick almost stalled again, but Dickie goosed the gas quick, and we rolled out of the parking lot, the car in low growl.

Old Man Fecteau, white-haired, tanned, and standing on the office steps, watched us drive off. He looked at us like he owned us.

◢

Denny banged a right, a left, another left, and the 'vette shuddered onto one of those back back roads. Kind of road that didn't see more'n ten cars a week, didn't get plowed when snow flew. A lonesome road — where you'd dump a body. We were miles out in the puckerbrush, somewhere north of Manchester but south of Concord, and it was about one in the morning. Didn't know where in hell we were headed. "Trust me" is what Denny'd said when he'd picked me up.

He'd pulled up to the house in the 'vette. I hadn't seen him since Stain and Pam's wedding, and for days I'd rehearsed what I meant to say to him; made myself sick with the thinking. But when he stepped out of the car all I managed was "Long time no see."

I couldn't — didn't want to — confront him. It's not that I'm afraid of him. My problem is that I think I understand him, and I knew that bringing up him and Pam Durocher wouldn't accomplish nothing. So I swallowed the poison I'd been steeping for Denny and let the subject of Pam Durocher drop without ever bringing it up.

Denny looked at me and, like he knew what was on my mind, said, "I might do evil things, but my heart is pure." Then he laughed and asked me to take a ride.

"Your ma's out," he said. "And Frank's still over to the County Farm. So what's the friggin' holdup?"

I'd learned better a long time before, but I went anyways.

It was a Friday night, but neither of us'd killed a beer. I could always tell when Denny was serious: he wouldn't drink.

"Couple more miles," he said.

Those were the first words he'd said in at least an hour. Whipping along back roads, we'd ridden from Granite in an easy quiet, windows rolled down, radio turned low to the Red Sox coming in from the West Coast. Late games from the coast were the best. The announcers, Ned Martin and Jim Woods, seemed to kick off their shoes and down a couple beers as they called the game, as loving and careful in the telling as some kid talking about his new girl; Ned and Jim knew who listened in at one in the morning.

We turned down a dirt road, the Corvette stuttering on the washboard.

The barn, like a warning, rose dark and alone from the middle of what should've been a field wild with corn. Instead, dozens of cars and trucks were pulled up to the barn, their chrome snouts pressed close: piglets sucking a sow dry.

Inside — the air thick with the stink of cigarettes, sweat, and stale beer — stood a boxing ring circled by bleachers, the movable kind you'd find at a high school football game. Ones that could be taken down quick. Me and Denny had ringside seats — the guy at the door knew Denny, and Denny slipped him a sawbuck to make sure he kept on remembering him — but while I sat there waiting for the fights, Denny had taken off.

"Got some business to tend to," he'd said. "I'll be back before the fights."

Denny never got me mixed up in his doings. But I wasn't stupid. I knew what was what out to his 'vette — pot (and maybe worse), guns, knives, stolen TVs. Even so, I made allowances for Denny and understood that some day there might be a price to pay.

I'd never seen them before, but both Bub and Frank'd told me about these bare-knuckle fights; they'd just called them "the Fights." Illegal as all hell. Binges of booze and betting. Crowd was familiar to me, though. I was practically raised on cockfighting and dogfighting. Same difference, 'cept in that barn the animals were men. It seemed Bub was always training fighting dogs or cocks. Where other kids' fathers took them fishing or to ballgames, I got took two, three miles deep into the woods, where I saw mutts and chickens rip the shit out of each other. My old man and his buddies drinking, yelling, and swearing.

Bub was a prick. But he told good stories about those fights; when he was telling a story, it seemed I could forgive him the world. There was one story I never got sick of hearing no matter how many times he told it:

"We're fighting the birds over to New Falls," Bub says, "and it's about two in the morning. Anyways, I'm taking a leak away from the action — one of those long, hard beer pisses that seems it's gonna last all night — when I hear somebody scuffing down the path. I look up and there walking towards me, I'm not shitting you, is Ted Williams. I'm so excited that my faucet shuts for a second. Ted sidles on up to me, unzips his fly, and there I am draining the snake with Ted Williams — the Kid, the Splendid Splinter, the Thumper, Teddy Fucking Ballgame! All six foot three of him.

"So I whispers to him, 'Ted, is that really you?' He laughs and claps me hard on the back, 'bout knocks me over.

"He spends the rest of the night with us, laying out hundreds of bucks on the birds. All the while he's there, this little weasel guy who's with him keeps saying, 'Ted, it's pretty cold. Don't you think you better put your coat on? How about your coat, Ted?' But Ted ignores him the way you do your old lady when she's on the rag."

Bub pauses. He takes out his wallet, opens it real slow, and slips out a five-dollar bill signed by Ted Williams. It says: "Bub, thanks. Ted."

"We didn't have no other paper," Bub says, "so he had to sign this."

When Bub took off on us I tore the house apart, looking for that fiver. But the bastard took it with him.

Anyways, I didn't feel too out of place sitting in that barn as it filled with whiskey-drunk, hard-armed guys whose hair was no-haircut long and who, in their delicate way, showed off tattoos of tits and snatch. My old man's kind of crowd, all right. But what got me were the scars. Those men, those pitiful shacks of God, rippled with scars: angry purple snakes; railroad tracks slashed across open skin; a razor-thin worm falling into the black of an empty eye socket. Stories written in a cruel alphabet that I understood as good as any of them; between Bub and the factory I'd been carved on pretty good in my time. They were men who understood blood and pain for what it was. A boxer couldn't have asked for a better crowd.

The fighters were pretty much what you'd expect: loggers, carpenters, truckers, bricklayers, mechanics. Strong men who'd spent their lives working hard and figured that maybe they could pick up a couple of bucks by decking somebody. Piss-poor fighters, though. Went at each other like wood axes — bar fights with no bar. Most of the fights lasted under a minute. Savage squalls, punctuated by the thump of flesh on flesh, that ended with a bloody body slumped to the mat. Then the rustle of soft, worn money, the money of poor towns, changing hands as the drunken crowd hooted and swore, belched and farted.

"Ain't this somethin'?" Denny asked, his face lit by the realest smile I'd seen on his face in months. "You can't tell me you don't like this."

He was right. The ring was small, the lighting bad, and the fighters crude as homemade furniture, but I couldn't take my eyes off 'em. I watched every Ferris wheel left and roundhouse right, the eyes swell and the noses burst, the sweat fly from a man's face as his head snapped back. There's something pure about two men fighting. With every fight I saw — whether in a boxing ring, at a bar, or at the factory — I figured I learned something new about the world; I even felt like that after my own fights.

Hitting is something women don't understand. To be hit hard in anger and to hit hard back is a lesson. And as stupid and simple as it sounds, you need to learn to hit back harder than you get hit. But it's that simplicity, that true balance, that makes a good fight.

I like to hit. I like to feel another body give, the blood rush to my head. Part of it, I guess, is that I was raised on violence; it got so that I flinched whenever Bub come near me. When I hit, I imagine it satisfies the anger that I see in my eyes every morning when I look in the mirror. I'm the kind of guy who'll stop and watch kids play baseball. But I'll stop and watch them fight, too; I won't break it up, neither.

"How'd you like to be up there?" Denny asked me.

"You kidding?" I said. "Those bastards are huge."

"Tell me about it," Denny said. "Some of those guys are here every week. But you ain't seen the best of it yet."

"This goes on every week?"

Denny nodded. He was the most relaxed I'd seen him in a long time. It was like he had nothing to prove in that barn; he knew that at least half the guys there could beat the shit out of him. They figured he was harmless, the wiseass kid who sold them reefer and whatever. Denny could just sit back, watch the fights, and get loaded; he liked it that way.

"Wait till you see this last fight," Denny said. "They got this racket going where they bring in some big ol' retard to fight this guy they call the Champ. Got a new 'tard every week."

Somewhere in his forties — hair gone gray, his once-hard gut unknotting — the Champ was a well-built boxer who wore a permanent roofer's tan. Couldn't go it with the young bulls no more, but he still had the fight in him. He stood calm, within himself. The bleachers shook when he was introduced, but he didn't look up. He barely nodded, a quick up-and-down snap — no wasted motion, nothing to be read into it — same as he would've given his barber if he'd seen him at the grocery.

They led the retard in blindfolded, a rope tied around his neck. He was a head taller than the Champ, and his square hands, fish-belly white, were the size of baseball gloves. They led him to his corner, whispered in his ear, him nodding hard, and untied the blindfold.

"My fucking word," I said.

Lloyd Hartford waved to the crowd, the same way he used to wave at the cars on Route 49, and people started laughing. A mean and ignorant laugh. A hey-ain't-that-retard-a-goddamn-riot laugh.

"Champ's gonna murder him," Denny said. "He don't stand a chance."

Seeing Lloyd like that, lumbering towards the center of the ring, knocked me off balance; my ears flushed with a shame I didn't understand.

Lloyd stuck out his hand to shake the Champ's. The Champ, disgusted, stared at Lloyd's hand like it was cancer, till Lloyd pulled it back.

The cowbell pealed to start the fight, which wouldn't end till one of the two men went down or give up. Lloyd stood stock-still in the ring's center, the Champ circling him the way a logger does who's sizing up a tree. Lloyd craned his neck to watch him. The Champ's first punch, a smart left, opened up Lloyd's right eye; the next one doubled him over; and the third straightened him up. But Lloyd didn't move, just stood there like he was trying to figure something out. If it wasn't for the blood sieving from his eye, you'd a thought he was trying to figure out what flavor ice cream to get over to Roy's Acres.

The Champ backed off, wary, the crowd already urging him to finish the job. His face all weasel cunning, he moved in again on Lloyd, who this time held up doubled fists to protect himself. The Champ flailed at Lloyd's clumsy defense — a pickax set to granite — but Lloyd rocked back, then forward, and crushed the Champ's jaw, then his nose, spinning him against the ropes. The unexpected always happens quick.

The Champ stared up at Lloyd — who looked as shocked as anybody — trying to draw courage from the blood he licked from his face. But he was afraid. The crowd, sensing that fear, fell silent as Lloyd clumped towards him. Somebody had fucked up bad.

◢

Crumpled, bloodied, the Champ lay at Lloyd's feet; even a retard can only be pushed so far. But that wasn't the end of it.

The crowd, every man Champ's brother, booed and finally chanted, "Retard! Retard! Retard!"

And Lloyd Hartford, the poor bastard, still stood in the center of the ring, paralyzed by his own stupidity and fear, a man trapped in a fire.

Denny said, "Let's get him out, Duston."

"Huh?" I said.

"Let's save him."

When I looked at Denny, I knew he was in one of his moods. It had snuck up on him the way Lloyd had snuck up on the Champ. Those animal eyes of his looked desperate, this side of pained. Denny didn't want to bail out Lloyd Hartford's ass; he wanted to get beat up, punished. Already, the whiskey-strong men were heaving from their seats and staggering towards the ring. "Retard! Retard!"

"No," I told Denny.

"Come on, Earl."

"I said no, goddammit!"

Frank always told me never to get into a fight I couldn't win unless there was good reason. If that'd been Denny up there, or Dog, or Stain, I would've done it. Lloyd, no matter how much I felt for him, wasn't a good enough reason.

The men climbed into the ring, their beer guts getting hung up on the ropes.

"Let's get the fuck out of here," I said to Denny, who — for once — gave in. He didn't like the odds.

*

"Mallory's still on my case," Denny said. "Can't believe his shit."

"He ain't even a cop or nothing no more," I said.

"Acts it."

"Swear he's never going to get over those watermelons."

"Bastard's getting on my nerves, following me all over like that."

Stretched out on the knoll that overlooked Swett's Pond, elbows planted in the ground, we were drying off after a swim. We'd driven there from the fights and were the only ones there. We were doing our damnedest to talk around Lloyd Hartford.

"All I know," Denny said, "is that Mallory's shit better cease."

Mallory was a pain in the ass. Seemed he spent more time tracking Denny than running his store. In the old days Denny would've just laughed at him, figured some way to piss him off even more. The Denny I'd grown up with had been tough, but he could laugh.

But something had happened to Denny, too, that night with the watermelons. Even though he'd let on otherwise, Denny'd been afraid when Mallory pulled the gun on him; I saw it. He hated Mallory for that, maybe hated himself more. And in his own fucked-up way, Denny had gone about proving he wasn't afraid: running dark in the Corvette, taking Pam Durocher on her wedding day. Folks in town said it was only a matter of time before he got caught breaking into one of those summer camps around the lake. There were stories going around town of windows smashed and doors busted open in broad daylight, of Denny selling dope out in plain sight at Al West's Cafe. Denny had always been hurting. Mallory'd made it worse.

I never made excuses for Denny, but that whole summer

— and after — I kept thinking on a story he told me once during one of our two-case nights. I picked at it like a scrap of pork chop stuck between my teeth:

I'm on him for leaning on Dickie's girl, Val. Tell him it ain't fair.

"What's this fair bull?" he says. "You want to know about fair? Couple summers before we moved to town, when we lived over to Pittsfield — I was about eight — my little brother Tommy wanders off one Saturday. Don't know how t'hell it happened, but he wanders off. And all of us are looking for him. After a couple hours, my folks call the cops, who're 'bout as useful as tits on a bull.

"Anyway, our next-door neighbors, the Watsons — they moved later that summer — kept an old frigerator in their dooryard. I must've walked by that thing half a dozen times that day. Never give it a thought. Then, towards dusk, I walk through the Watsons' yard again and I look at that frigerator like I seen it for the first time. It was one of those short ones, you know, with the rounded top.

"I start bawling, standing there in the middle of the yard. Couldn't move, couldn't do nothing but cry. I knew Tommy'd smothered to death in that frigerator. Finally, my old man hears me crying and comes running, but real careful not to spill the bottle of Pabst he's carrying. I think he meant to smack me, till I pointed at that frigerator.

"He runs over to it — and I can tell he doesn't want to open it — and finally he pulls open the door. But he doesn't even catch him. He drops him. My old man lets my dead brother fall on the ground."

My thoughts were as still and dark as Swett's Pond, the kind of mood that only Denny could put me in.

"You know," Denny said. "A lot of it's Mallory's fault

that all those Mass-holes are moving up here. Guy's a fucking traitor. Man, I can't stand all those Mass-holes. They're changing the town. I bet there's not five people from town that own a place around the lake no more. God, I hate those bastards. Strut around town. Act like they own the place. I only steal from *them*, you know. I know you don't like to hear this shit. But it's true. I only steal from those pricks.

"Know what I'd like to do? Take my old man's rifle one Friday night, climb one of those big old oaks down to the town line, and pick off every goddamned car with Massachusetts plates that has the balls to cross into town. Yeah, that's what I want. I want to kill their men and screw their women so hard that I drive my bone into their brains."

The wind rose quick, strong, mugging us, creaking the trees, and slapping the water onto the beach. Lightning tongues darted, crackled. Thunder as low and mean as Denny's voice growled off towards the south. Lightning flashed again, electric barbed wire fencing in the night. Thunder grumbled louder, closing in.

We waited for the rain. It wouldn't come.

Flat on our backs, we watched the ragged scars of electricity stitch the sky, heard the thunder thump closer, near as loud as the factory at full blast.

That wind felt so good, we couldn't wait for the rain. Rain. We'd been needing rain for weeks. So many dry places to fill. Still, it wouldn't come.

It stormed something fierce, though — *Boom! Boom! Boom!* Swett's Pond boiled as the sky burned with lightning; the wind cast sand devils. A lightning bolt sizzled through the sky, close enough to touch, and crashed into the woods across the pond. The explosion vibrated in my stomach.

"Rain, you bastard! Rain!" I shouted.

It hurt my eyes to look up into the sky, that pit full of electric snakes, hissing, snapping, squirming, striking. The thunder roared and groaned, a dying giant.

Then it was over.

Like that. The wind died to a breeze, the thunder echoed far away, and the lightning flickered like a little kid's sparklers.

Over. Dry heaves.

I looked over at Denny. He was asleep.

11

THERE WAS NOTHING FINE about Frank Sargent's hands. They were hard and square and scarred: a two-inch tear on his left thumb where he'd fumbled an ax; two, three rips on his ring finger where his wedding ring, long since gone, had snagged on something or other and about tore his finger off; small scars, from punched-out windows and punched-in teeth, salt-and-peppered his knuckles; a gash that stretched from the tip of his little finger across the meat of the right hand to his wrist, a long time ago, some bar, a drunk with a switchblade. He rubbed the reptile ridge of calluses just below his fingers; those calluses were as much a part of his hands as the fingernails, knuckles, and scars. So he sat on the edge of the steel-frame cot in his cell at the County Farm, holding up his hands, turning them, studying them. It hurt to keep the fingers straight, and he let them sag into claws. Like that, his hands reminded him of the junk man who'd come around when Frank was a kid, when he picked the dump.

He first picked the dump the summer he was nine, when

he and his mother lived upcountry in the tarpaper shack in Thomson. Only thing that shack had to recommend it was that it was just a five-minute walk down Canaan Back Road from the dump.

The dump. Amid the sizzling hills of garbage and scuttling rats lurked little treasures: birdhouses, comic books, copper wire, tires, returnable tonic bottles, bicycle skeletons, Christmas tree ornaments. At the end of most every day, Frank and his buddies swooped down on the dump, scuffing through the mess of brown paper grocery bags, stumps, and dirty orange flames — bitter gray smoke and ash swirling, shifty-eyed gulls in full complaint wheeling overhead — the boys' movements punctuated by the pop of exploding bottles and the .22 rifles of the men out rat hunting. The boys scoured the dump, harvesting anything that might put an extra nickel, dime, or quarter in their pockets. They heaped the loot onto homemade wagons they'd built out of scrap lumber and two-by-fours.

It was the junk guy, who came around twice a month from April till October, who put the money in their pockets. He mattered. Money was tight. "It's so bad, Frankie," his mother used to say, "that I got to make that buffalo on the nickel take two shits." Most everyone in town knew what it was like to go on the relief.

Still looking at his hands, Frank remembered that the last time he'd seen the junk guy was right before he and his mother moved out of Thomson so she could take a waitress job down to Wolfeboro:

Morning comes hot after a cold hard rain the night before, and the air holds that heavy hothouse smell of mugginess and flowers in full bloom. Steam rises from the ground; the summer-green leaves drip — lazy, leaky faucets; a wasp pauses at a wormy mud puddle; and Frank's sneakers soak as he kicks through the sopping grass. But the sun works hard. Frank and his friends are sweaty by the time they finish lining the driveway with their bulging wagons.

Frank always feels lightheaded on junk guy days, finds it hard to set his mind to the sorting when he knows the junk guy might only be a mile or two away. It's the same feeling he gets waiting in line at the movies, or waiting for the teacher to hand back a paper that he knows he's done a good job on. Later on, it'll be the feeling he gets before he opens the first beer of the day.

He's counting tonic bottles — Mr. Frostie, Moxie, Old Kerry — when he hears it: the groan of the mulish Dodge being shifted, the clatter of the big scales bouncing and banging as the truck growls down the road. They all stop what they're doing and tune in to that sweet sound. Frank's mouth cottons, his palms grease up, and of a sudden he has to take a pick-ed wiss, but he holds it.

The truck, closer now, bumps along the cracked, buckled road, the scales clanging louder, bolder. The steamy July morning sheds its dreamy skin as the air shimmies with the tolling of the scales. A dog barks, two sharp reports. The birds nag and scold, old men roused from a late-morning nap. The truck lumbers around the corner, its wide wood box already half stuffed. The big Dodge grinds and squeals as it lurches to a halt in front of the boys, the scales smacking into each other like the Three Stooges brought up short.

The boys close in. The junk guy, a ghost behind the dirt-streaked windshield, looks to be fiddling with a notebook and pencil. Frank steps back, admires the Dodge. Its wide chrome grille, rust-pitted, reminds him of the grin of an old man who's proud to still have his stumpy teeth. The cab and box are painted a shade of red just right for a fire truck or a sleigh. But it isn't some impotent professional paint job. That truck had been attacked by that red paint, which eddies around the Dodge in thick, murderous strokes. Just as striking is the truck's size. Bigger than a pickup, it gives off a sense of slow, indomitable strength. It's like someone's mounted four tires on a big old snapping turtle, splashed it with red paint, and set it loose on the road.

The driver's-side door swings open, and the junk guy steps out and down. "Mornin', boys," he says. "Hotter'n a witch's tit, ain't it?" The boys laugh.

He — Emmie Lete's his name — could be thirty, or he could be seventy. He wears a blue baseball cap (Agway Feed & Grain) pulled low, just over his black eyes. His face is filthy, slick with the same coat of grease and grime that plasters his dungarees, red flannel shirt, and work boots. The boys wonder how he gets so dirty, wonder whether he ever takes a bath. They covet his job. But it's his hands, rough and horny with nails the black of potatoes gone bad, that take Frank's breath away. The junk guy goes no more than five-five or five-six, skinnier'n a gartersnake, but each of his hands could palm a watermelon. Those hands, they bend unnatural at the wrist into fetal curls; his fingers are wilted flowers. He always pulls on work gloves before he picks over their harvest of junk, and Frank swears it takes him a good five minutes to straighten his hands enough to put them on. Then the junk guy, this side of panting, says, "Well, boys, what've you got for me t'day?"

"Psst, Frank. Can I come in?"

Frank slapped his hands to his sides as if his mother had caught him jacking off. He looked to the cell's open door. Only Edgar Collins.

"Come on in," Frank said.

It was after supper, the cell dusking up. But Frank hadn't bothered with the light. Edgar eased into the chair across from the cot, where Frank sat still as if waiting for something.

"How y'doing?" Frank asked.

"'Kay," Edgar said, lighting up a generic-brand cigarette. "They got done picking the jury today. Trial's s'posed to start tomorrow." He took a drag on the cigarette, coughed. "Want one of these?" he rasped. "Good for what ails ya."

Frank shook his head and said, "Who's the judge?"

"Some broad. Crescento, Crescintinio — I don't know."

"Consentino. Sent me here and put me on the program. She's okay."

Edgar heaved a sigh. "I don't know what the hell's going to happen," he said. "Sometimes I don't even give a shit. Ever feel that way?"

"All the time."

"Y'know," Edgar said, "if it weren't for drinking and women . . ."

"Yeah," Frank agreed.

They got the quiets — Frank staring at his hands, Edgar sucking down his generic — and the deepening dusk filled the cell. Out to the highway, a siren, a trailer truck shifting down.

"I just don't know," Edgar said. "I truly don't."

"Don't feel lonesome," Frank said.

Edgar shrugged, gouged at the paint on the chair arm. He held a paint speck up to his cigarette; it wouldn't burn, and he threw it on the floor.

"You work so goddamned hard your whole life so some fat fuck can sit on his ass in some office," he said. "And you're told that's the American way. But you try to forget about it, try to get something steady, get paid decent so at least you got a pot to piss in — if nothin' else. And comes the day you drag your ass home from work and she tells you to get the hell out, tells you y'ain't no good, and that she doesn't want you coming round no more. She wants a divorce like some country western slut. She kicks you out the house, takes another man into your bed, and the cops tell you that you better not show your ass around no more, or they'll throw you in jail so fast it'll make your balls spin. The American way. I've been getting it up the ass from the American way since I can remember. Know what I mean, Frank?"

"Yut," Frank said, nodding. "Yut."

"So you start driving by the house every day now," Edgar said. "The one that used to be yours. You see the kids playing in the yard. You see a car parked there that you ain't seen before. And you get some kind of acid burning in your gut. You can feel it chewing on you the way a dying dog'll chew on its own leg to get the pain out. You know that pretty soon, unless you do something, y'ain't going to be a man no more.

"So finally one day you just can't take it no more. That acid's burning hateful little holes in your skull. And you go out and get crocked. And you buy some shells for that shotgun you've had since your old man give it to you when you were twelve years old. You go to the house one morning when the kids are in school, when you know the cunt is sitting in the kitchen eating her goddamned Hostess doughnuts, swilling coffee, and watching some shit on the portable TV that you give her two Christmases ago. You sneak into that house — your house — into that kitchen, and she's still there in her housecoat, and you get a hard-on, most useless hard-on you'll ever get in your life. You call her name so that she jerks quick from the TV, looks at you, that sweet mouth open just so.

"And the next thing you know, her cinnamon doughnut is rolling on the floor towards you, and you kick it at her. You take out a couple more shells — just to make sure — but all you can think about is that goddamned doughnut rolling at you.

"When it's over, when you've silvered up, when you know what you've done, you know what the real kick in the balls is, Frank? The acid don't dry up. It just gets worser and worser. And sometimes you wish you still had that old shotgun, because it wasn't her you should've shot."

Edgar lit another cigarette. The match flickered, lighting up his puckered red face, the gross alky nose, the greasy white hair. Frank felt like he was looking at a long-lost brother.

"What's going to happen?" Frank asked.

"Nut house," Edgar said. "I *was* crazy."

"Could've been me."

"There's a shitload of us, Frank."

Frank gnawed at his lower lip, stared at the floor. "Know what's crazy?" he said. "Being cooped up here and all, I feel freer than I ever did."

"Man's got to be left alone," Edgar said. "Guys like you and me, we need to be left alone. Be far away. Even a small town closes in on us — a steady job, a woman. You get crazy, start drinking."

"Makes things bearable," Frank said.

"Till it starts making 'em worse."

"Edgar, if they let me and you be, let us go upcountry to the woods, we'd never bother nobody. I worked the woods, best times of my life."

"You've said."

"You worked hard and honest."

Edgar asked, "Can we listen to the ballgame?"

"Okay by me," Frank said as Edgar clicked on the radio.

The radio spit static; they could hardly hear Ned Martin's voice. Frank stood up and looked out the barred window: a newspaper danced in the courtyard as the sky seethed with rolling gray clouds. He heard Edgar, settling in for an evening's neighborliness, fire up another generic.

◢ 12

We knocked off half an hour early. Johnson was in Old Man Fecteau's office downing a few, so what the hell. Keegan, one of the truckers, had said he had "something special" for us — being that it was the day before Granite's Old Home Day celebration and all. We handled bad shit at the factory, but once in a while we got drums by mistake brimming with good stuff: juice, peanut butter, shampoo, rustproofer. Andy took home a whole drum of prune baby food one time. Keegan put drums like that aside and let us know, and that's why he'd asked us to meet him at the burner.

Me, Dickie, Dog, Murphy, G.I. Joe, Marcel, and Lurch had all pulled up drums and were sitting around, shooting the shit. Marcel and G.I. Joe worked a grubby joint.

"How can you smoke that in this heat?" Lurch asked them.

"Makes you cool," G.I. Joe said. "When I was in the Marines. Those hot days down south. Cool."

G.I. Joe grinned, took another hit. Him and Marcel, the goddamned stoner brothers. They did crazy shit. Marcel swiped dead rats from the lunchroom traps, painted them red, white, and blue, and strung them from his paint booth. This is the same guy who filled Lynch's Thermos with piss, paint, and pepper. G.I. Joe wasn't any better. He ran the water cooler through the blaster — "Impure water," he said. And another time, hands on hips, he pissed his way around the outside of the factory — "Keeping the dust devils down."

Lurch shook his head. "Give me a rack of hooters any day. Beer's better'n that dope stuff."

Murphy said, "That's what makes that Braley kid so useless. Smoking all that LSD in the shithouse."

"Sure could use a cold one right now," Dickie said.

"That's what the fuckers are probably sucking down in the old man's office right now," Dog said, jerking his thumb towards the air-conditioned trailer.

"Naw," Lurch said. "They're just sucking on the old man's dick."

We laughed, real laughs, the kind of laughter meant to tell the factory, the heat — hell, the world — to go fuck off. Laughter that makes you feel a little more human and a lot less of a screw-up. The good laughter of a bunch of guys who don't give a shit no more.

Goddamned Lurch. Tall as a tree, wide as a bulldozer, and strong . . . Let me tell you. One time I seen him pick up, single-handed, a new motor for the blaster and press it. That motor was bigger than a V-8 engine. Heavier, too. When Lurch walked down the road, he blocked out the sun.

"Anyone got a butt?" Murphy asked, coughing, his voice radio static. Murph always stunted his coughing fits with a cigarette, the old hair-of-the-dog route.

"Sure." Marcel grinned, offering the joint.

"Not that bullshit," Murphy said. "I want a real cancer stick."

Lurch flipped him a Kool. "What kind of fag cigarette is this?" Murphy asked. "Don't no one smoke Camels or Luckies no more?"

"Work in this friggin' hole," Dickie said, "you don't need no cigarettes."

"Tell me about it," Lurch said. "Doctor keeps telling me to quit this place. I says to him, 'What'm I supposed to do? Let my kids starve?' He don't have no answer for that."

"Andy quit," Marcel said. "Hear he's making out."

"More power to him," Lurch said. "Don't know how he's doing it — if he is. Maybe he's just a better man than me. But I doubt it. I looked for other jobs. I know what's out there."

"Ain't nothing," Dog said.

"Unless you want to push broom, kiss ass, and get paid squat," Lurch said.

Murphy sucked in his Kool and blew the smoke out his nose, dragon style. "That's some fag cigarette," he said.

"What're you doing this weekend, Murph?" I asked. "Got plans?"

"Yeah," he said. "Stay home and watch the ballgames. Old lady's got to work."

"Sox're looking pretty good," Dickie said. "Beat the Orioles last night. Two games out now."

"Give 'em a chance," I said. "Ain't August yet."

"Fucking Sox," Dog said. "Bust your chops every year."

"Fisk's the only one got any balls," Lurch said. "And that's 'cause he's from New Hampshire."

"Homegrown!" G.I. Joe screamed. "Fucking-A! Homegrown!"

Lurch kept on like he hadn't heard. "Rest of those guys are pussies — major league touch-holes."

"Aw, come on," Dickie said. "What about Yaz? He busts ass."

"You heard me," Lurch said.

"Man's going to be a Hall-of-Famer," Dickie said.

"Had one good season," Lurch said. "Nineteen sixty-seven, when they won the pennant. Don't give me this Carl Yastrzemski bullshit."

"Maybe things'd be different for the Sox if Tony C. hadn't a been beaned," I said.

Tony Conigliaro was the Red Sox right fielder in 1967, and on one muggy August night that summer his face got crushed by a wild fastball. I listened to that game on the radio, but I can still *see* that sonuvabitching pitch ride high and tight and drop him like a shotgun blast to the head. Sometimes still, I'll be listening to a ballgame and, of a sudden, I'll see Tony C., his face swollen, a black lumpy bruise gnawing at his skull. To me, in the summer of '67, that black bruise was the end of the world.

"You guys know where I can score some firecrackers?" G.I. Joe asked. "I want to get some Black Cats and cherry bombs."

Dickie said, "Going to war?"

"Yeah, no shit," G.I. Joe said. "Watch out, anthills. You know, those little fuckers catch fire and start screaming."

"Think Dirty Willy's selling 'em," Murphy said. "Sold some last year, anyways."

"Dirty Willy," G.I. Joe said.

"Where's Keegan?" I said. "We ain't got all day."

"Probably off looking for Braley," Lurch said. "Guy's useless. Had him working with me and Homer on covers. Spent half my time looking for the lazy cocksucker. Told Johnson that if he didn't get him out of my department, I'd close the bastard up in a drum and forget about him."

"Too many guys like that," Marcel said, talking dope-slow. "Want to get paid. Don't want to work. I might screw the dog some, but I work, goddammit."

"Don't know," Murphy said. "I been working in factories since I was sixteen. Most young guys nowadays ain't worth the powder to blow 'em."

Dog yawned and said, "Who wants to bust ass in this pit?"

"Ain't the point," Murphy said. "You get paid, you work. It's that simple."

"I ain't gonna break balls for an asshole like Johnson," Dog said.

Murphy shrugged.

"Hey, there's Keegs," Marcel said. "'Bout fucking time."

Keegan and Braley were wheeling a full drum out of Vinnie's toolshed; it sloshed when they set it down. Keegan lifted the cover, and Braley set Styrofoam coffee cups and quarts of Old Kerry's ginger ale on the cleanest drum he could find.

"Remember that pure alcohol from last Christmas?" Keegan said. "Got some more last week. Been saving it for today; two-hundred-proof fireworks."

"Aw-right," Marcel said, snapping off a gap-toothed grin.

"Fucking-A!" said G.I. Joe. "Stuff'd give a baby crotch hair."

I shivered. That stuff went down like splinters. Even cut with ginger ale, it had burned my throat and teared my eyes. Some of those guys slurped it up like beer.

"Don't do us no favors," I said to Keegan.

"Come on, Duston," Braley said. "You pussying out?"

"Braley," I said, "I want shit from you, I'll squeeze your head."

Couple of guys laughed.

"Oh yeah?" Braley thought he was hot shit. He puffed out his chest — queer rooster was more like it.

"Yeah," I said, standing up, arms loose.

The guys stayed put. I stared at Braley. He wore a black T-shirt that was too tight. His arms, which were thick enough, were carved with tattoos of skulls and bare-assed women; he had a face as memorable as corn flakes. Wouldn't look at me as he shifted from foot to foot. All he had to do was back down. I wasn't looking to fight. I was sick of fighting. I hated being on edge, always having my guard up.

Don't get me wrong, I ain't against a fight; like I said before, I like to hit. Sometimes two guys just need to knock each other's brains out to set the world right. But a fight needs consequence. Before two men lay into each other they better goddamn know why they're doing it. Having a fight with a Braley made about as much sense as napping on the yellow line out on Route 49. The Braleys of the world shit on their honor and yours too.

"Well, Braley?" I said.

He looked at me, then at the rest of the guys — hoping, praying that someone would step between us. They were quiet, except for the ones laughing. Braley, with his alligator mouth and hummingbird ass. Denny had no use for him. It was Braley who run out on Denny once over to the Hotel Maplewood and let him get slaughtered. When most guys are rocking on their heels and doubling their fists, Braley's balls are slinking up towards his throat and his feet are finding the door.

But a Braley is dangerous, the kind of guy has no pride. He'd take a beer mug to your head, knife you, shoot you. A man with no pride and no balls is more likely to kill you than a man who does.

Finally, Braley said, "So you want to fight, huh . . . well, crawl up my ass and fight for air." He smirked. No one laughed.

"Fuck this," I said and turned my back on him. I'd won without throwing a punch. Cheap enough. "I'm thirsty. Let the pussy make his jokes."

We bellied up to the alcohol drum, ignoring Braley. There was a war on at the factory — against Old Man Fecteau, Johnson, and everyone like them. Every worker, whether he liked it or not, fought in it. But Braley wasn't a boss, and he sure as hell wasn't one of us. He was in no man's land. We figured he wouldn't last the month. He watched us, caught in between what to do next; even his breathing seemed hesitant. He knew he was out.

"Good stuff, huh?" Keegan said.

"Depends," I said.

My eyes watered without me even taking a drink. I found the ladle in my hands — "You first," Keegan said, "you deserve it" — and dipped it into the drum. Stuff looked like water but had the kick of Frank Sargent's boots. Poured it into my ginger ale and stalled, sniffing it. Once I got a whiff of that sick-sweet ginger ale smell trying hard to hide the alcohol's raw fumes, my throat tightened and my gut knotted; I remembered the hangover from the last time, two days of someone hammering a drum and I was crammed inside. I'd sworn never again. Even so, I brought the cup to my lips. As I did, out of the corner of my eye I saw Braley running, rushing at me like wildfire in the burner. I tensed, but all he did was grab my drink — "Fuck's the holdup?" — and gulp it down. I couldn't believe it. Braley trying to save face, a face I was about ready to rearrange. But that ain't what happened.

Braley's cheeks turned fire-truck red, his legs stuttered,

and his eyelids fluttered in a mothy way. "I can't see!" he screamed. "I can't see!"

A couple of guys laughed. Good joke, Braley. Maybe you're not as big an asshole as we thought.

"I can't see! Help me! Can't see!"

The laughing got louder, Braley's face burned redder. We didn't stop laughing till Braley, running blind and arms windmilling, rammed full tilt into the burner, gashing his forehead. He fell backwards into the chemical muck, blood gushing. He flopped and thrashed, the dirt working into his skin and clothes, mingling with the blood spattered on his body.

"I'm blind! I'm blind! I can't see!"

The sun seemed hotter than it had all day. Braley squirmed on the ground; we watched. Marcel and G.I. Joe stoked another joint; Dickie and Dog hooked their thumbs in their pockets; Keegan leaned on the alcohol drum; Lurch scratched his chin. We'd paid our quarter to see the sideshow, and we were deciding whether it was worth it. Braley started to cry and lay flat on his back, his hair slick with the blood that was still spilling from his forehead. Tough luck, Braley.

He looked like something spewed out of the burner, covered with the sooty soil, paint that'd pooled on the ground — and blood. His tattooed arms were red with it. The tattoos looked stupid. You don't need skulls and crossbones and swastikas and snakes gouged into your arms in green, yellow, and red ink when you're bloody. Blood's a good tattoo, the real tattoo.

"Help me."

Me and Keegan looked at each other, traded cold shakes of the head. I thought of the turtle I'd seen splattered on Meeks Road the month before. I'd felt worse for that turtle than I did for Braley. I couldn't even imagine myself there on the ground. Sure, Braley drank my poison, but I figured he went blind because he was Braley. We all shit the bed in the end, but the Braleys of the world tend to do it sooner rather than later. If I'd have drunk that stuff it wouldn't have hurt me because I'm Earl Duston. Something special. Nothing could fuck me up, 'cause I was going to live to be a hundred — at least.

"I'm blind." TV static.

Keegan and Armand wheeled the alcohol drum to the pit and spilled it out. Braley whimpered. It's all gone now, Braley. Sshh.

We stared, somehow disappointed. We'd knocked off early for nothing. The guys' grimy faces didn't look any different from how they looked when they worked. Same tight mouths, same clenched teeth — same face, too, for when they ate, when they drank; it was probably the same when they fucked.

Murphy threw down his Kool in disgust and went to call an ambulance.

◢

Frank stood at the barred window, his arms folded on the sill, chin resting on his hands, staring so hard towards the woods that he might have been praying. He didn't even hear me walk into his dusky cell.

"Frank?"

He turned dream-slow, and we stood there in the twilight looking at each other.

"You come," he said finally.

I nodded, and the silence swallowed us the way the fog does the low ground out to Route 49. This wasn't our easy porch silence. It was the quiet after a car crash, like we'd reached down each other's throats and ripped out our tongues, leaving only bloody stumps — desperate but unable to talk. We couldn't even dredge up the small talk, that false weight we all give each other day in and day out. I'd driven all the way out to the County Farm to see him, and we had the talking dry heaves.

There's this dream I had all the time when I was a kid:

It's deep night and I get woke by a crackling sound, like someone's crinkling cellophane from a pack of Camels, and I see this tongue of flame licking at my window. That's what's making the noise, and right away I know the house is burning down. But I can't move, can't even scream. One invisible hand's pinning me to the bed and the other's clamped over my mouth. All I can do is twist my mouth into wordless shapes and watch the flames blossom at my window.

After a while, Frank shrugged helpless-like and walked back to his window.

I drove too fast on the way home.

13

OLD HOME DAY morning I woke with the sweats — hot, dirty water that as soon as it seeped out, turned cold and gave me a chill. I'd dreamt of me and Azalea fishing Center Marsh:

She snags a big one that gives her no fight at all. We haul it in, dead weight, and it's Braley — hooked through the eyes. He flops in the boat same way he did at the burner, and Azalea picks up a sawed-off baseball bat and lets him have it in the head a couple times.

That's when I woke up.

I sat at the kitchen table eating Cheerios while Ma nested out to the porch and took in "The Beverly Hillbillies" on the TV. She never used to go on the porch, but she'd practically moved out there since Frank got sent to the County Farm. She'd dragged her chair out, the TV, hung curtains, laid a rug. The porch had been Frank's and, through him, mine. But Ma had taken it away, and that ticked me off. On "The Beverly Hillbillies," Granny shrieked, "Jed! Jeeeed!!!" Ma snorted her closed-mouth laugh.

We kept out of each other's way, Ma and me, two mean dogs sick of the fighting. We had nothing to say to each other that hadn't already been said. We'd yelled it all out — about Bub, Frank, everything. It was best not to raise those ghosts again.

Usually I was long gone before she got her ass out of bed in the morning, and I generally come in after she'd gone to sleep. Since Frank had gone, there'd been at least half a dozen different cars parked in the dooryard when I came home at night. Sometimes, the cars were gone when I woke — burned off like morning fog. Other times they were still there when I left for work. I never saw no one — raspy voices in Ma's room, a few squeaks of the bed, is all. Car I saw most was a white Caddy with upswept razor fins and a wide front grille that smirked rust. I was surprised it was even on the road. The windshield was spiderwebbed with cracks; it was rusted worse than most of the steel drums stacked outdoors at the factory — the red-brown rot eating at the creamy white body; the driver's door and trunk both dented; one taillight smashed; and clear plastic covering one of the glassless back windows. Inside: floors ankle-deep in beer bottles; shredded seats, the white stuffing poking through; in the back window, one of those hula-girl dolls listing to one side on a broke spring. That was the best car.

I don't know how Ma spent her days. Guess she drank some, watched TV, puttered around the house. I never asked her. And as long as she run the house decent, I wasn't going to. On payday I left her enough money to buy groceries, plus a little extra. I felt like I was the grown-up and she was the kid, not that she — or Bub — ever showed me how a grown-up should act. I suppose she could've taken a job. But with the drinking and all, she would have been shit-canned pretty quick. Besides, she always said she couldn't work. Said she was too used to having a man — when she got drunk, she said it "may-ann," whining the word — take care of her. I wondered what'd happen if I cut her off, didn't give her no more money. Probably would have moved out, shacked up with one of those cars I'd seen. I couldn't have done that, though. For all the shit, I still owed her. What? I don't know. She got me born. That was something. Hard to complain about that.

Crusty jumped up on the table and eyed my cereal. He'd pretty much healed from that fight, but he'd picked up a limp somewheres. Goddamned cat. He stalked my cereal, whiskers twitching, nose flaring. The way that cat acted, you'd a thought I was eating mouse for breakfast. Finished, I pushed the bowl towards Crusty and he danced back, suspicious, sniffing, then leaned forward and licked the bowl, his red tongue darting up and down like the needle on a sewing machine.

I ruffled his ears and stood up. Ma laughed again and I heard a banjo picking "The Beverly Hillbillies" theme song. Ma sang along, her voice granite humping granite: "Once 'pon a time there was a man named Jed, poor mountaineer, barely kept his family fed . . ."

I shrugged and walked outdoors. Hot.

I spent the day in the swamp, hoping I wouldn't see Azalea, nobody. I wanted to be alone, wanted to think. But things only got more tangled and murky. As I walked, I thought about them all — Ma, Frank, Bub, Stain, Pam, Braley, Azalea, everybody — tried to figure what in hell was going on. But it all was as unknowable as the swamp. And it all kept coming back to Denny. I could figure myself out only after I figured him out. But Denny . . . I knew the paths that led to him, but I didn't know him. And beyond Denny, beyond all those people, stood me. They lugged around pieces of me, but the pieces were hidden, buried somewhere dark and deep.

My thoughts always turned on me in the swamp. It dredged up the goddamned past, which was always laying for me. It was the same that afternoon. Before I knew it, I was a kid again:

It's an August afternoon. The kind of close day where the air's wet-sponge heavy, and I walk the half mile to the small country store to cuff a pound of bologna because Bub needs sandwich meat for work. I keep checking my pants pocket like I expect a five-dollar bill to somehow show up there, but it stays empty. They say that money burns a hole in your pocket; let me tell you, being broke burns a worse hole.

A wood-frame rectangle, the store squats on cement blocks; it isn't painted, still has the rough edges of raw lumber. Only reason it stays open is because it sells beer to minors. Inside, it stinks of stale beer, cigarettes, and the sawdust that's settled on the tops of cans of Dinty Moore beef stew, corned beef hash, and Spam.

Gary, a man whose face is as rough as the lumber used to build the store, runs the place. Sucking down Marlboros, he plays the big shot with the high school kids; he drinks beer with them and tells dirty jokes. He nudges the pink slab of bologna back and forth on the whirring meat cutter, the slices sloughing off like dried skin. Slices are so thin you could read the *Union Leader* through 'em; the meat lasts longer that way.

My hands are sweating when Gary's about finished, my gut churns. I haven't told him that I want to cuff the meat, that I don't have no money. I don't want to say it to him, don't want to say it in front of the two high school guys slouched against the wall drinking beer. I wish Bub'd cuff his own goddamned bologna.

Gary drops the bologna on the counter in front of me; the thud and the processed smell of the meat make me sick to my stomach.

"Anything else?" Gary asks.

I shake my head.

"That'll be . . ."

I look at my sneakers. "Uh, can I, uh, cuff that?" I about whisper.

"Can't do it," he says, sweeping the bologna quick off the counter like he thought I'd steal it or something. "Can't do it."

I stand there, ears and eyes burning. It's what I've always been afraid of, me having to find out that my old man's credit's no good.

"Y'ain't got no money, ya can't get no meat." Gary laughs mean, winking at the two high school boys.

Scuffing my way home, I choke on the shame and hate stuck in my throat. Later, Bub beats the shit out of me for screwing up.

I shunned Center Marsh — Azalea's haunt — and angled off north and east across the B & M tracks towards higher, drier ground. Somewheres up in there — who could say where exact? — Cedar Swamp's magic petered out and gave way to plain old Granite, which eventually became the Kingsbrook Woods, which is to say, woods like any other.

I hadn't spent much time out that way. It was the deep swamp that deviled me, kept me coming back to Cedar. Not those woods. Tramp too far from Center Marsh, I figured, and the woods got too ordinary, became friggin' Boy Scout woods.

Still, those woods beyond the tracks belonged to Cedar Swamp, I knew, and maybe, just maybe, they were worth the hike. So, like always, I slogged ahead. I figured that maybe those new woods'd strip me of my worries, or at least take my mind off the goddamned horseflies welting my neck.

Damn, I hated horseflies: brown, bastard triangles that'd nip at your scalp, get tangled in your hair, then fly away after you smacked 'em. A mosquito had the decency to stay squished once you whacked it; a horsefly would only get pissed and try to poke your eye out. No rhyme nor reason to 'em, the crazy bastards. With a single mosquito there was the ritual; patience and timing paid off. But horseflies were dive bombers — quick, mean, tough. Miserable little pricks. I did have to admire them, though. They were trying to make their way in the world, same as anybody or anything else.

Sunlight spilled into the abandoned quarry and . . . vanished . . . sucked into water as black as the granite cliffs that surrounded it. And up on those cliffs sat Azalea Kelley, dipping one of her plump white toes into thin air like the water was just inches away instead of the good twenty to thirty feet that it was. There was no getting away from Azalea Kelley that day; she waved me on up to where she perched.

Till that afternoon, I swear Azalea hadn't spoken a hundred words to me in my whole life, and most of those had been of the yes and no variety. Everything I knew about her had come from watching her or from listening to folks in town. But when I sat down next to her, she started right in. It was like she'd been waiting a long time for us to talk.

"That's old, old water down there," Azalea said, pointing a cricked finger at the still quarry soup. "Drought's sucked up the younger water. That water there, it hasn't seen the sun in forty, fifty year. Been down there so long, doesn't even think it's water no more. Thinks it's stone."

She stared into the black water as she spoke — if granite could speak, it would sound like Azalea Kelley — like what she had to say was written there. I studied her face, a Colonial that needed a good sanding and a fresh coat of paint.

"This pit here, Earl," she said — it was the first time she'd ever spoke my name and, for some reason, I blushed — "this pit is why we are called Granite. It's the very first quarry. You'd think a town like Granite'd make a big to-do about this first hole we dug. But Granite craves its secrets. Oh, yes. What do you suppose we'd find, Earl, if we siphoned off all this water? What do you think?"

I shook my head.

"Somethin' that needed buryin' in the dark woods," she said. "That's a fact. Oh, there's trouble in these woods, in all Cedar Swamp. Gets worse and worse all the time. Remember this, Earl Duston: when you go after black granite, you throw out half what you take and consider yourself lucky."

"Azalea?" I asked. "What in hell are you going on about?"

She looked at me. A trick of the sun made it seem she was crying black tears.

"Somethin's wrong in the swamp, Earl," she said. "Don't know what it is, but somethin's gone wrong. It trembles in my belly and I can sniff it in the night air. I had to tell somebody. That's why I followed you up here."

"Huh?"

She forced a smile, said, "Azalea is the swamp, Earl."

She'd managed to string me up somewheres between being spooked and being p.o.'d. "What're you getting at, Azalea?"

"I don't want you coming to the swamp no more, Earl."

"What?"

"I don't think you should come to the swamp no more. Call it an old woman's second sight."

"You're fucking nuts. What do you want? The whole swamp to yourself? You jealous or something? This swamp's as much mine as it is yours."

"Somethin's going on."

"Something? Something?"

Azalea grunted herself up, stared down at me; her eyes had turned snapper-black. She said, "I don't lie, Earl Duston. I've never told a lie in my life. Want to know what happens to folks who can't lie? They get hounded into Cedar Swamp."

I knew that she'd been telling me what she thought was the truth. But I knew, too, that it was only her truth.

As I sat there on the quarry cliffs, staring into the true guts of Granite, I thought of how the barrel factory sang late at night, rang with drum song as steel expanded and contracted. A pure sound, steel-drum blues; steel — strong, dependable steel — tugged this way and that by hot and cold. Something to wonder at, something to almost make you smile, the drum factory singing — or an old woman who claims to be Cedar Swamp.

When I got back to the house, I decided to go to the carnival uptown on the Plains. If I'd stayed home, I would've made myself sick with the thinking. I washed up, put on my good dungarees and a white shirt, and took off.

I stood out on Route 49 near the factory — the tar soft and warm through my sneakers — facing the traffic, thumb out. I could have walked to the Plains, but I didn't want to get sweated up. Cars coursed by steady, some heading to the carnival, most speeding to the North Country for the weekend. It was getting towards sundown, but it was still plenty light; none of the cars had their headlights on. Some cars slowed, but most of them ignored me.

Now you got to have a certain frame of mind to hitch. You can't get pissed, no matter how many cars pass you by. No one's stopping for someone who looks pissed. Second, you got to be pushy. When that car's coming up the road, step forward, smile, flash that thumb, look like you just got out of church, and stare that driver right in the eye with the most honest face you have. Even if he doesn't stop, he'll feel guilty as hell. There are times when no one's going to stop for nothing. Then you just have to put up with it. What gets me ticked are the people who speed up when they see a hitchhiker; it's like they think the hitcher's going to jump in the road, grab the car by the fender, and stop it. Folks don't have to stop, but they don't have to be snotty, neither.

The way they were passing me, though, I was starting to wish that I could stop cars with my bare hands. I'd been standing out there a good twenty minutes without so much as a nibble. Getting pitty, too. Kids pointed at me and stuck out their tongues; old ladies glared, their root hands choking the steering wheel; and some asshole in a Ford pickup threw a firecracker at me, hand-grenade style over the cab's roof. I popped him the finger.

Finally, a blue Dodge Charger slowed, flashed its directionals, and bumped to the side of the road. I got that little shiver a small victory will give you and ran to the car. But as I opened the door, the guy tromps on the gas and peels out — left me there holding my dick and inhaling burned rubber.

I was pretty goddamned fed up. But then I saw Denny's Corvette humping up Route 49. I grinned and knew I had a ride.

He didn't stop.

Didn't even slow down. He looked at me — right through me is more like it — like I wasn't even there. Weren't no one with him. He just hauled ass by. I turned, watched the 'vette till it dipped below the hill and out of sight. Man, I couldn't believe Denny Gamble's shit. It was right then that I knew it wasn't my night. If I'd had any brains, I would've gone home and waited for the Red Sox to come on the radio. Instead, I started walking towards the center of town.

The Ferris wheel stuttered to a stop, my car rocking at the tip-top. From up there I saw the whole center of town — not that it made much sense to me — all the way to both ends of the Plains, that swatch of green that started at Bessie's Lunch and stretched about half a mile, past the fire station and town hall, up to the high school. Around Old Home Day, Smokey's Show of Shows came to town and took over the Plains. And at midnight on Old Home Day itself, after three days of the Ferris wheel, Beano, two-headed cows, and the like, the Granite volunteer fire department set afire a tower of gasoline-soaked railroad ties; a junked car, usually some rust-gnawed shitbox from Floyd's Junkyard, sat on top the bonfire, which every year drew thousands of people from around Sanborn County. The patch on the Plains where the bonfire burned each year had been scorched black for as long as anyone could remember — like the small cancer on your good-lookin' aunt's beak.

I was still at the top of the Ferris wheel — from up there the mob overrunning the Plains looked like chunks in some thick, steamy stew — and glad for it. A ride on the Ferris wheel could make you feel like you'd just conquered Mount Washington, even if you were the lowest scum in

Sanborn County. I closed my eyes and thought of Mary Tucker. First time in two years that I'd gone to the carnival without her. Thinking of her brought on the smell of fried dough soaking the air as we walked hand in hand, the two of us alone in the crowd. Brought on the feel of us riding the Ferris wheel, looping around — from bright lights to the peak of darkness — as the seat swayed. But those memories pissed me off too, because they took something important and made it seem stupid. Thinking on Mary made me tongue-tied, but all I could dredge up were sick-sweet boy-and-girl pictures that didn't mean squat, didn't begin to explain the sadness that I about gagged on sometimes. Mary Tucker had made the bullshit bearable, and I didn't know how to say that to myself or nobody else.

Right then, I didn't know why I was there, why I'd bothered with the carnival, the Ferris wheel. Bending over my seat's restraining bar, I looked straight down. A line snaked from the Ferris wheel booth, wound around the Beano tent, and disappeared; the man running the Ferris — a black guy in a tight T-shirt — hunched over the diesel engine that powered the wheel, a wrench in his hand.

As I stared down — the Ferris's rainbow lights flickering and sputtering, the other cars rocking and squeaking — I wondered for a split second what it'd be like to jump, to spread my arms and hug the earth, to open my mouth and gorge on dirt. What would it be like to fly past the cars below, where old couples gingerly held hands and buttoned their sweaters another notch against the night; where hot teenage boys — ice in their hearts and fire between their legs — clawed at their girls' tits, the girls glaring but shifting to help the blind, groping paws? To shoot past the small children whose faces were buried in Mommy's or Daddy's lap? What would that be like?

Pretty fucking stupid, I said to myself.

The Ferris wheel shivered, shook, and creaked forward, bringing me back down to earth.

I leaned on the fence near the Ferris wheel, followed its lazy looping path the way I would a mosquito's. I don't know whether I liked looking at the Ferris wheel because it reminded me of Mary, or because I just liked looking at it. In its guts it was only another smoke-farting machine. But it floated in the night, a bright bobber cast upon a dark pool. The other rides — the Octopus, the Scrambler, the Dive Bomber — were noisy, violent, and ugly. They wouldn't've been out of place at the barrel factory. But the Ferris wheel . . .

Well, it's like this:

One day I'm working, and a drum scrapes in from the burner. As I shove it to Andy, a butterfly dances up out of it. A big butterfly, big enough so it makes me jump back before I see what it is, fall yellow and marked by thin, black stripes. It hovers unsteady, wings dipping, this crazy splotch of yellow caught in the steel-dust rain. I grin because it tickles me, the idea of a butterfly rising up out of a steel drum like it was some 55-gallon steel cocoon. I decide to save it — catch it, carry it outside — but as I sneak up on it, the little bastard flutters towards the blaster and Andy, who grabs at it and misses. Dirty Willy swats at it with his shovel, whiffs. They go back to work, but I chase the butterfly. I'm not giving in.

The butterfly wobbles towards the ceiling, a dying flame as it flickers into the tangle of cable and wire, the shoots of filthy sunlight. I track it as it weaves across the room, no one paying attention, and finally drifts lower to settle on a rat — fresh-killed, wet blood at the corners of its mouth —

from Marcel's paint booth. I pick up the butterfly, careful not to hurt its wings as it thrashes in my hands, and walk to the back door. I open my hands and the butterfly skitters away, fades into the dead, gray trees.

Imagining the Ferris wheel at the drum factory is like remembering that butterfly. Same difference.

I took a bite out of my burger and washed it down with a slug of Moxie. Good ol' Moxie. Might've tasted like root beer with the roots still floating in it, but it was good for what ails ya. Actually, it made me feel good to hang out there — better'n one six-pack good — sopping up the carnival air: that humid mulch of spitting grease, diesel exhaust, cotton candy, sweat, Brylcreem, and the smoke of spent firecrackers. When it comes to carnivals, you can have your rides, games, and sideshows. Let me have that sweet, heavy carny stink.

I'd never figured Kate Mallory out. We'd been friends in school, tumbled into drunk gropings a couple times. But there'd been Mary — "Earl's smart-assed bitch," Kate used to tease — and there'd been Kate's old man. She might've moved out of his house and got her own place, but Kate was still Freddy Mallory's daughter. And here she had me about pinned up against the fence near the Ferris wheel, so I couldn't help but take in her snug-assed jeans and lipstick-pink tube top.

I guess what it comes down to is that these girls — Mary, Kate, a couple others — scared me. They seemed to know what they wanted. But their lures, whatever ones it was they used, made the gawk in me break to the surface so that my skin flushed and I didn't know whether to stand up or sit down. With the guys — Dog, Stain, Denny — I could be me, shoot the shit or shut up as I saw fit. But the girls, as much as I liked them and wanted them, caused me to stare quiet as slow fire kindled in my pants. There was some mystery that I didn't get. Even with Mary it'd been there. It wasn't much different from when I was in grammar school. I opened my eyes one day and discovered Judy Elliott.

Judy Elliott was plainer than mashed potatoes. But I had a crush on her. She had but to look at me to bring on the stutters and the turn-reds. She sat in front of me in Miss Yansick's fifth-grade class. I felt like I could've sat there for days and stared at Judy's November-brown hair, the back of her pale neck, the slope of her shoulders. But that crush, it wasn't something to be spoken.

There was something else, too. Something back then that I'd called fatal. I didn't know where that word had sprung from, but it rang right. Like I said, I'd never said nothing to nobody about that crush, especially not to Judy herself. But there she is one yellow spring morning when I look out my bedroom window. She's across the road, behind the big oak — practically a marrying tree — peering at our house. Her. Judy. And for a split second life's exciting, dangerous. All because Judy Elliott, the vanilla girl of my daydreams, is hiding across the road.

"What y'been up to?" Kate asked. "Ain't seen you in a while."

"Nothing much," I said. "How 'bout you?"

"I'm a hairdresser over to the Perm Palace in Plaistow," she said. "Went to school for it. In Manchester."

"What's the old man think?"

"He can go fuck himself, for all I care. Know what he does every night? Drives over to my apartment and parks in the driveway for ten, fifteen minutes like he's still a goddamned cop or something. Piss me off. Bangs his Spam, for all I know."

We laughed, almost touching, her hair brushing my face.

Even though I'm gabbing with Kate, Donna Gonyer lurched into my thoughts. No mystery to her. Taught me a lesson once, though. That's all. She used to clean in town, same as Ma did sometimes, and about every morning when I was a kid I'd see her stumble up the road towards the Plains. To me, she was what most folks must've meant when they spit out the word *retard*. Her black hair, bristles on a cheap paint brush, was clipped in a raggedy bowl cut; her lips were thick as Schonland franks; and one leg was shorter than the other; so was one arm. She wasn't that old, maybe sixteen, seventeen.

Donna cleaned for Denny's mother once a week. One Wednesday — her day at Denny's — when I was twelve or so, me and Denny are looking for his football. We walk into his brother Brian's room without knocking, and there's Brian, buck naked, laying on top of Donna Gonyer, who's just as naked. Brian jumps up — sex slick, smelling of b.o. and come — and looks mean at both of us. Doesn't say a word, but his look — the smoldering behind the eyes, the hard-set jaw — tells us to keep our goddamned traps shut, tells us that he'll hurt us if we ever squeal, hurt us bad. Donna Gonyer looks up at us from the hardwood floor, her nubby legs tented, and whimpers, "Come here. Come here, hon-nee," as she scratches her swampy crotch with a spaz hand.

Brian bangs the door behind us, the windows rattle. Donna pleads, "Bri-an, hon-nee. Come here, hon-nee." We hear the smack of a flat hand striking flesh, once, twice, three times — fastballs whomping a catcher's mitt. Then nothing.

"Still at that damned drum factory?" Kate asked.

"Yeah," I said.

"Uh-huh."

"Thinking of quitting, though."

She smiled, looked at me, up at the Ferris wheel. "Let's go, Earl," she said, holding out her hand. "Come on."

I grabbed Kate's hand — part of me still holding out for Mary — and, drunk on the carnival, the two of us ran hand in hand towards the Ferris wheel.

Planted smack in the gut of the Plains, the bonfire reared up some forty feet — begging to be gawked at, maybe even prayed to. And come five-till-midnight, Granite Fire Chief Tommy Tucker III — or Tommy Tucker the Turd, as we used to call him — vaulted the fence that circled that tower of railroad ties. Tommy claimed that he'd quit as fire chief on the day he couldn't jump that fence no more. But we all figured he was as full of shit as his name; there weren't no other Tommy Tuckers in his family, never had been.

A gas-soaked fuse tailed from the bonfire, and Tommy, showing off in full firefighting gear — he even had a goddamned ax slung over his shoulder — galumphed towards it as folks drew up to the fence. Making it look like some kind of magic trick, Tommy struck a wooden match one-handed, lit the fuse, bowed to the crowd, and lumbered off. The fuse spit and sparked as the fire crawled towards the top, where a deceased '63 Falcon sat. Behind me and Kate, the carnival rides still revved and roared, kids still shrieked and laughed. But to my ear, as we watched the fire climb its ladder, it seemed quiet enough to hear a pebble plop in a deep well. When the fire closed in on the top — Kate squeezed my hand; she was stronger than Mary — the crowd rushed towards the fence, and me and Kate got shoved to the very front, our knees nudging the wood slats. The fire burrowed into the darkness under the car. We got pushed harder, the fence bowing inwards. A couple of wild pokes with my elbows produced some breathing room.

Then, with the *whoom!* of an oven lighting, flames bloomed that overran the bonfire and Floyd's shitbox car. Crowd whistled, clapped, and hooted like they was at a dog fight. Kate squeezed my hand again. I squeezed back.

Flames swirled around the ties the way water will around the legs of a dock; whips of fire darted in and out of the gaps as smoke and ash drifted into the night sky, smothering the Plains. Sparks floated up till they winked out like dead stars. I saw monsters in the fire: burning snakes, fiery tigers and wolves, flame trees, Bub's face, then Ma's, Frank's, Denny's. Shifting, changing every few seconds to forge new fire creatures. I suppose that if I'd looked hard enough, I could've seen God, or maybe Ted Williams. But I was never any good at seeing things like that. My face crawled with the heat, same as it did out to the burner, and my hand sweated in Kate's. Fire flickered in her eyes as she stared, as stone-silent as the folks pressing in on us; it seemed the bonfire'd parched their vocal cords. But no one turned away, and the carnival deadened. Hanks of smoldering wood thumped to the ground and sparked; the car's steel sang. Kate's cheeks and forehead shined red and made her look even prettier. I kissed her nose — muffin-warm.

"What do you think?" I asked her.

"Sshh," she said, raising a finger. Then she kissed me — a kiss asking patience — with hot, dry lips. I needed a beer something wicked.

Finally, 'bout half an hour and one goddamned baked Earl Duston later — didn't I get enough of that shit at work? — I heard the bottom ties groan, then shift, as the bonfire caved in on itself, the twisted hunk of car slipping free and nosediving into the Plains, railroad ties burying it. The bonfire laid low, not any more special than some burning heap of garbage you'd find over to the dump. The crowd, bone-dry and wore out, understood that and turned away real quiet, almost funeral-sad — maybe feeling cheated. The bonfire had let them down again. It had stood there on the Plains for some two weeks, looking impossible tall, so important. But when it come down to it, after that split-second thrill of the thing blossoming in flames, all it was was a bunch of goddamned burning logs that smoked up the air and left a black spot on the Plains. But by the next year, they'd forget. They'd be back.

A tire rim had popped off the car during the fall, and, glowing white hot, it rolled towards the fence, slow, steady. I tracked that rim the way other folks'd gaped at the fire. It's funny what we see and don't see. When the rim hit, it fell over and wobbled like a coin flipped on a table. It was so hot the fence caught fire; a couple of firemen ran over and put it out.

Kate tugged at my hand, kissed me. She could catch afire any second.

"Let's go," she whispered fierce. "Let's go."

◢ 14

WHEN THE SLAMMING CAR DOOR woke me, I started. I had that smothered feeling of waking in a strange room before I remembered I was in Kate's apartment, sleeping in her bed. I looked at the clock-radio on the night table. About four in the morning.

Kate sleeping reminded me of pictures I'd seen of unborn babies — all curled up like snails — in their mothers' stomachs. Mary had slept that way, too, thumb near her mouth. It was hard not to think of Mary. You compare without knowing: the range of sighs, eyes open or closed, the weight of their breasts, how deep the nails bite. Me and Kate'd talked, laughed; she'd seen the scars on my back, understood without saying, and touched them, kissed them. It had been too long since Mary. It wasn't even the sex so much as the warm of another body that wanted to be close to mine, that I wanted to be close to. When you're worked hard and don't have much money, there ain't much can make the world seem right. It don't surprise me that poor people have so many babies.

Kate slept sound — strong, deep breaths. As I looked at

her, at the smooth curve of that bare back, there was something that wanted to make me cry. Some kind of deep night sadness all mixed up with longing, feeling protective. I would have killed for Kate Mallory right then, done whatever I could to keep her from hurt. All that, just because we'd fucked each other once. What a spell, making love. I saw it in Frank, that protective urge. When he wasn't drinking, anyways. One time we're all in the kitchen, me and Frank sitting at the table, Ma leaning against the stove. She turns away, walks towards the front room, and her apron strings are burning. Frank jumps up, just about knocking over the table, and claps out the flames with his bare hands. Just like that. Ma acts like it's her due. And there's Frank, the poor bastard, running cold water over his burned hands.

About to fall back asleep, I heard voices — voices that sounded almost familiar. Couldn't make out the words, but they had a pissed-off edge to them, and that was what goosed me wide awake. Kate didn't even rustle. I slipped out of bed, snuck towards the window at the other end of the long room — the only room in Kate's place — and nudged the curtains open a slit.

Freddy Mallory stood in the driveway, right below the window, arms out to his sides, looking like a man trying to sell somebody a piece of swamp. He was talking to Denny.

They were alone, two shadows backlit by the streetlight at the bottom of the sloped driveway. But I didn't need no light to tell Denny and his cocky, hands-in-the-pocket pose. Or Freddy Mallory and his gut, which he kept touching, petting it like a lucky rabbit's foot or suchlike. Mallory fidgeted and paced as he talked to Denny, who stood hunter-still, not buying a word of it. I wondered how long it'd take Denny to get tired of Mallory's mouth. It ticked me off that

Denny looked for fights, though I loved to watch him go at it. He was so quick, almost never got hit. I'd win a fight, but I'd take some shots. But Denny . . .

One time over to the All-Night Stand this huge mother — must've been six-four, 220 pounds — swings at Denny. Before you can blink, Denny blocks the punch, knees the guy in the nuts, rattles some teeth, and rams him head-first into the bar. Most people in the place didn't even see it. Denny had that instinct for the quick, nasty job.

Denny moved closer, almost touching-close, but Mallory backed off. He hadn't figured out that Denny'd been stalking him, not till Denny'd worked him up against the split-rail fence that ran along the driveway. Denny didn't lay a hand on him — guess he just wanted to devil him — but you could tell he was talking real serious, because Mallory kept nodding his head, a kid getting reamed out by his old man. Mallory didn't run, though. Give him that.

Denny finally turned away and started down the driveway. Mallory, brave of a sudden, followed and wagged his finger at him. I figured Denny to bite it off; he didn't take that kind of shit from nobody.

Denny turned slow, pivoting like a lazy basketball player, a knife balanced in his left hand. I wished right then that I'd stayed in that warm bed with Kate, that I'd never looked out that window.

Even in the heat, I shivered. I knew in my balls what was what, but I buried that knowing quick and told myself that Denny only meant to scare him. That's all. Make Mallory shit a brick. Just another game, and I could watch without meddling. Lies — while Mallory backpedaled up the driveway away from Denny, who waited till Fat Freddy Mallory stumbled and fell.

I ain't had it easy, and I thought I knew something about how hard people'll use each other. But I realize now that I didn't know nothing till I saw Denny Gamble tear Freddy Mallory apart.

Denny stood up, brushed off his dungarees, and ambled down the driveway, a man walking a dog. He laughed, a get-down-on-your-knees-and-drink-the-blood laugh that, if you're lucky, you'll never hear once in your life. Then he was gone.

I was sure Mallory was dead. The fact was in Denny's walk, the laughing. I was just as sure that Denny was going to get his own self dead soon. Mallory was an asshole. But he was a bigshot asshole. The cops would figure out pretty quick who killed him. Denny wasn't the kind to be brought back alive.

Know what I should have done? I should have called the cops right then. Woke up Leon George and told what I saw. That Denny Gamble had killed Freddy Mallory. How do I know that, Leon? Well, I just happened to be over here screwing Fat Fred's daughter when my best friend shows and slices Freddy up. That's all.

But I wasn't calling no one.

You know, all I had to do was open that window. That would've stopped it. But I let Denny play it out. Sometimes there aren't any excuses.

I simply remember this: Mallory crawls towards the house; I hear his gut scrape the tar. Denny lights a cigarette, watches him the way you might watch a pretty girl walk by. He shrugs. Knife in hand, Denny walks over to Mallory, kicks his head, which snaps to the left, then lurches back to the right. Kicks it again.

My best friend. My very best friend.

No man deserves to die the way Denny did Freddy Mallory. That's not the right way to kill. Doesn't take any balls to knife a defenseless man.

I shivered again, glanced at Mallory's body — a still

lump in the shadows. Denny's latest job, his latest success. I walked back to bed. Kate hadn't moved. Looked at the clock-radio. Twenty after four. I crawled in. Kate was so warm, so alive. I was winter inside. Right then, all there was was the waking up, the sneaking to the window, Denny and Mallory arguing, the knife — each stab, Mallory, Denny . . . round and round in my head. Goddamn you, Denny. Goddamn your hide. I could've saved him, I thought. Could've. More bullshit.

I saw that dead pond out behind the barrel factory that time when we were kids. That dead, scummy water. And I knew Denny hadn't wanted to be saved, never wanted to be saved. He knew what he was doing. I was just there to watch. From the erasers aimed at the teachers' heads to the dead pond to the drugs and the break-ins and the fights to screwing Pam Durocher on her wedding day to killing Mallory. I was only along for the fucking ride. I'd been hearing that laugh, that shrivel-your-balls laugh, in one way or another since I'd known Denny Gamble. Too many times. Seen that crazy I-don't-give-a-shit-for-the-world look of his. The chin out, the wiseass smirk, the animal eyes — all hiding something. All those paths that led to Denny didn't make sense. Didn't go nowheres. And I didn't get it. All I knew was that I'd still do anything for the bastard.

I cried. Heavy sobs that shook me, made me gulp for air. That bastard. That stupid bastard. The lump in my throat hurt, the tears steamed. I imagined that the tears were scarring me, eating at my face, that they were acid more wicked than anything at the factory. A factory boy's acid tears.

Kate woke up. Was my crying louder than her old man's dying?

"Hey, what's the matter?" She yawned, touching me, her voice dreamy.

"Nightmare," I said. "Just . . . just a bad dream."

She was no fool. There in the half light she gave me a don't-give-me-that-shit look. "Come here," she whispered. "Don't cry. Come here, Earl.

"Yes, that's it. Sshh. Come here.

"Is that better? Is it? Yeah. I thought so. Sshh."

◢

One December, the lake ice come in black. Which is to say, it come in clear and took on the cold black of the winter water it skinned. The old-timers, holding forth at Bessie's Lunch, called it "nigger ice" — spit out the words, really; said you couldn't trust it the way you couldn't trust a secondhand potbelly stove in a cold snap. They said some poor bastard was bound to fall through before the season was out, and it sure as hell wasn't going to be one of them, 'cause they weren't doing no ice-fishing till that ice clouded up — turned the color of blind eyes.

I didn't much believe those old farts. But there was something about that black ice that did make my breath catch. First off, veined as it was with frost, it reminded me of those fancy, black-granite gravestones over to the cemetery; it was like someone had taken one of those big stones, melted it down, and smeared the black soup all over the lake. Even worse was staring down into the ice, watching what stirred in the black. Of course, Denny liked that part:

Me and him are in the middle of the lake and Denny's on his hands and knees, squinting, his snout almost touching the ice.

"Earl! You gotta see these weeds way down," he says. "They're so cool! It's like there's dead people down there, but all you can see's their hair waving in the water."

I want to skate, but I give in. Like always. Then the two of us are gawking through the ice into such a blackness it seems it could open up and swallow us. It looks so poison to me — a lake gone dead — that I jump some when I see a pair of pickerel drift by. And before the fish fade into the black, I'm ice-fishing again with Grandpa Ora — I'm no more than four or five — and my feet ache from the cold like I'm barefoot on broken glass, and the pickerel, weedy-looking bastards all teeth and bones, are cordwood-stacked on the ice. But their frosted gills, flecked with blood, are still flexing, and I burrow my face into Grandpa Ora's tobacco-smelling coat so I don't have to see the dead fish breathe.

That same winter, me and Denny find a snake froze in the black lake ice. Denny sheds his skates, hacks two-fisted at the ice with their blades. "Come on, Duston!" he shouts. "Let's get that bastard!"

More than half an hour later we pull the snake out. It's stiff and brittle; frost shines on its black scales and its hooded eyes. "Look at that mother," Denny says. "Ain't that something?" He bites it. He lays into that ice snake's neck something fierce — but blood bubbles out Denny's mouth, drips off his chin, stains the snake's dead-white belly, the ice. Denny's busted a tooth.

"Son of a fucking bitch!" he roars; then, laughing that laugh of his, he scalds my face with a stream of blood shot tobacco-juice style through the new gap in his teeth.

That was the true dream I dreamt after I saw Denny kill Freddy Mallory.

◢

At first, the banging took on the shape of Frank Sargent building a chicken coop; then it changed to me unloading a truck at the factory; then, Denny taking a sledge to Mallory's Fruit & Real Estate.

I shot straight up in bed, chest tight, ears buzzing, head throbbing. Somebody was hammering at the door, bellowing wicked. But Kate was already there, unlocking it — the bed warm where she'd slept.

Walt Gonyer, the old buck who lived downstairs, stood in the doorway, heaving, his eyes scared-dog wide.

"He's dead!" Walt blurted. "Deader'n a goddamned doornail!"

You could tell that he'd needed to say it quick as he could. He'd been ripe with the knowing, barely able to keep it in, like a drunk who has to take a wicked piss. Once said, he calmed some.

"Who?" Kate said. "What're you talking about?"

"Your old man." Walt panted. "Out to the driveway. Just found him. Dead, I tell you."

Kate narrowed her eyes, pursed her lips — someone thinking over a hard but knowable question — and glared silent at poor old Walt, who'd expected a bigger rise than Kate gave him. He looked almost resentful that she hadn't at least started to cry.

"Didja hear me, girlie? Your old man's dead! Some bastard kilt him!" He yelled at Kate the way you yell at someone who's hard of hearing.

She said, "I'll call Leon."

They stood there in the doorway for what seemed a good five minutes. Finally Walt — all flustered and wheezing — stomped off.

I fell back into bed. Walt's saying it had made the killing fresh again. I was almost surprised that Mallory's body really was laying out there in the driveway. I hadn't even figured out before why someone would be pounding at the door that early in the morning. In just a little over an hour of sleep, I'd started burying what I'd seen, brought in the emotional backfill that lets you get by from day to day. But Walt'd swept that fill away. Denny and Mallory squirmed in my gut.

Without looking at me, Kate rustled into bed and gentled her head to my chest. I held her, knowing I was in over my head, and looked out the window. A little after six, and the blood-blister sun had edged just over the tallest trees behind Kate's place.

Hot again. No rain. Sun still putting it to us. A pissed-off sun, one we weren't used to in Granite, bearing down on us, on the land. Streams and ponds had shriveled to fish-smelling mud patches; the river ran so low that the summer canoe race'd been called off; farmers worried over their fields the way a new mother frets over a fevered child; the volunteer fire department feared a forest fire equal to the Great Fire of 1891, which'd burned up a quarter of Granite's woods — 'course that hadn't stopped them from touching off the Old Home Day bonfire, moneymaker that it was; wells were watched and wells ran dry; dust devils taunted; men, women, and kids, lugging jugs and pails, lined up at dawn and dusk to draw water from the town pump out back of the Baptist church down near the lake; the town looked to the sky the way Mallory must have looked to Denny. But the sun blazed as fierce and grim as Denny had. Folks told stories of snakes taking to the cool of their houses' stone foundations, of pigs and cows gone mad, of children crying all day long, of sleepless nights spent praying for rain. It seemed the heat would grind the land to dust, then the people.

Kate stared at the ceiling. Right then, it seemed enough that she knew. There was nothing we could say. Her father was dead, and she knew I'd seen Denny kill him.

Gentle, almost shy, she put me in her dry mouth. After I

got hard, she climbed on top of me. She whispered, "Make me a baby, Earl. Make me a baby."

She didn't call Leon till after I left. "You leave now," she said, kissing me. "You do what you have to do. I'll take care of this."

I brushed by Walt on my way out. He didn't even look up from where he sat huddled on the back steps — his puffy red face stuck between crying and not crying — killing a six-pack.

◢ 15

THE WALK HOME wasn't no big deal. I picked up Pop Cosgrove's railroad off Britton Road, the boonie patch where Kate lived, and headed towards home. A wooden crossbuck still guarded the rusted tracks, which'd sunk into the road; when those tracks were laid the road probably had been dirt.

Pop Cosgrove had mined iron ore out of Granite Lake — mostly before World War II. One of the things Pop did was build a spur line between his mill and the Boston & Maine tracks beyond Cedar Swamp. Pop had his own engine and a couple of freight cars he used to haul the ore out to the B & M every day. When the mill closed, some time in the early fifties, the spur had been left to rot. But even after Pop Cosgrove sold his holdings in town, gathered up his money, and moved away, folks still called it Pop Cosgrove's railroad; hunters mostly used it when I was growing up.

And if you were patient, peered into the trees in just the right way, you could uncover a spur off the spur, where the Cosgrove & Granite line had abandoned its mighty locomotive, a one-hundred-ton dragon that'd been strangled by the woods: its sixteen wheels seized to the tracks; asbestos guts were spilled on the ground in coarse heaps; its once-black skin was checkerboarded by rust, moss, and lichens; squirrels, bats, and mice squeaked in its innards, scuttling among the train bones; the mud wasps hovered at attention. The past put in its place.

Even though no trains had run on it for more'n twenty years, I liked the fact that the spur and the engine were still around. Say "Pop Cosgrove's railroad" to anybody in town, and right away they knew what you were about. Those rails were history forged in steel. Back in '38, Jeff Robie killed a monster twenty-point buck on those tracks — biggest buck ever taken in Granite — and derailed Pop's train to boot, having barrel-assed into that goddamned deer late one night when he was half in the bag; during World War II, Pop organized a citizens' militia — mostly kids, women, and one-armed jacks — and, for a time, called himself Major Cosgrove; Grandpa Ora worked over to the iron mill when he got done with school — for most Granite men it was that or the quarries — and his brother, Malachi, died there, having got himself drunk and drownded one payday. "Your Uncle Malachi was a sweet, stupid man," Grandpa always used to say. So many tales waiting to be told. Seemed that if you followed those tracks as they curved into the woods, the stories'd never end.

That sense of history, all bound up with a set of railroad tracks, was a comfort to someone like me, who came from a family — except for Grandpa when he was alive — that may as well've been a worm-gnawed rowboat set adrift in the Atlantic fucking Ocean. Pop Cosgrove's railroad, Cedar Swamp, the Marrying Tree — those things spoke to me of beginnings, middles, and endings; they carried the weight of meaning, anchored me in the world. If it'd been left to Ma and Bub, I probably would've spent my days hiding in the dusty dark under my bed.

Anyways, those tracks would take me close to home, save a couple miles of walking.

When me and Denny were in junior high, he had a couple of dirt bikes that we'd race through the woods. Sometimes we rode Pop's railroad, our asses jouncing up and down as the bikes' knobby tires bounced over the ties. Denny in the lead because he always took the faster bike. I suppose that most anything in Granite could've reminded me of Denny if I'd wanted it to. I swear, we knew every goddamned back road, every washboard logger's trail, every path — no matter how small. We'd gallivanted on foot, bicycled, dirt-biked, and, finally, driven in his cars.

I couldn't get free of Denny; he throbbed in my head.

I focused on the rail bed, trying to shove Denny away, and took in the green moss, full and soft as Crusty's fur, that grew between the gray, punky ties; yellow, red, and purple flowers with pinhead blossoms dotted the moss. Six-inch rail spikes and black clumps of pitted, melted steel lay on the crushed-stone bed, mingling with empty beer bottles, cigarette butts, the red and green of spent shotgun shells. The woods' low branches hung down, brush-kissed the rails, and in some low spots swamp, with beavers' help, had flooded the tracks. Important once upon a time, that stretch of railroad had become an unraveling thread going nowheres; it fit my frame of mind perfect.

I breathed deep and held the thick green smell of the woods in. That sweet odor was almost a cure for the heat, for Denny, and it cleared my head some. I unbuttoned my shirt, sweat-stuck to my back. But when you come down to it, nothing could've made me feel any cooler, any better.

*

Ma still wasn't home. But I couldn't face the shack alone, so I headed back into the swamp — screw Azalea Kelley. I could lose myself there, follow one of my favorite trails, one that was just wide enough for a body. I didn't feel like traipsing to Center Marsh, though. I wanted to filter through shadows and grays, chew on the night before. Center Marsh would've been too bright, sun splashing on the water. I needed the dusky inner woods. I'd never told anyone about the swamp — not Mary, not Ma, not Frank, not Denny. Nobody. It was mine alone, and I didn't want to share it. I began to understand why maybe Azalea'd asked me never to come back. But as I passed through the woods, I started to believe that Denny was there in the swamp — over that rise, up that tree, in that gully — waiting for me, maybe hiding under water in one of the marshes, breathing through a reed like in the movies. I knew it was bullshit. Some kind of wishful thinking. But I couldn't shake the feeling and it pushed me through the swamp like I was on a hunt. Not one with guns and hounds and flashlights. A different kind, one I didn't quite get. The woods seemed darker than they'd ever been, the trees thick and black, the sun, for all its bastard strength, shut out, only a hint through the dense leaf cover — the sun seen in a dream. I walked faster, jaw set, fists doubled. I wanted Denny to show, to rise from the swamp shadows. I wanted to whale on his ass for a good week. Then I wanted to shove him under Azalea Kelley's shack and make him live there till he goddamn well grew up. Stay till he understood in his balls that life wasn't some mosquito game where you swatted away a man's life just like that. I felt darker than the woods. Denny had dug an icy black hole in my gut, and filled it with acid.

*

I'd been walking more than an hour, working myself into the swamp, when I decided to pull up. I found a fresh-cut stump, probably some tree Azalea'd taken, and sat down — bent forward, elbows on knees, hands clasped loose, staring at the ground — the woods quiet except for my breathing. Till I sat, I hadn't known how beat I was. It was like the sitting had shut down the engine that should have run out of gas hours before.

I tried to hold Kate Mallory in my head. Couldn't. When I thought of her, my eyelids sagging, Denny elbowed his way in. Picked up a twig, broke it. The *snap, snap, snap,* which seemed to carry for miles, woke me some. I rolled the pieces in my hand dice fashion, flung them on the ground, and snatched up another twig.

Snap. Snap. Snap.

◢

I tramped out of the swamp in late afternoon with the sun hinting it might give in some, and there was Leon George, setting on the shack's back steps, reading the *Union Leader* and sipping ice coffee from a Thermos jug.

"Earl."

"Leon."

"Your ma's not home," Leon said, "so I come out back for the shade."

Me and Leon sized each other up. But you know, I wasn't bothered to see him waiting there; it was almost a comfort. Leon was one of those square-jawed, gray crewcut guys who still believed in a firm handshake and plain talk. After everything he'd done for us, what with Frank and all, I trusted him.

"So how's your ma?" Leon asked.

"Same-o, same-o. She ain't missing Frank much."

"Yut." Leon nodded. "Yut." He paused, then said, "Saw her over to the Eagle's Club last night with Roland Simes. Not to talk to, though."

"Rollie Simes, huh?"

Leon shrugged, lit a Marlboro, and said, "Just wanted to let you know that we'll be wanting to talk to you in the next few days. Ain't no big deal. We'll be talking to everyone. You know how it is."

I nodded. No sense in bullshitting around the bush. Leon thought the same. He said, "Ain't had a killing in town since Hector was a pup."

"When was the last one?" I asked.

"Oh, that was an awful thing. Happened in 'fifty-nine, I think — anyways, Ike was still president. This woman, Helen Burford, went crazy and drowned her three little kids in the lake. She died a couple years back — over to Concord, in the nut house."

"Never heard about that."

"Folks in town don't talk about those kinds of things much. Least, they pretend they don't."

"Yeah, no shit."

Leon took a long drag on his butt, drawing smoke hard into his lungs, and washed it down with ice coffee.

"How long you lived around here?" I asked.

"At least three times too long," he said.

"What do you mean?"

"Oh, I don't know. People ain't as friendly as they used to be. Seems like everyone walks around with a bug up their ass or something. Then you got all those people who've been stepping all over everybody else for years and years — it's in the blood. You got the Bakers, the Georges, the Hetzels, and the Tuckers. They always been saying what's what in Granite since anyone can remember. That mightn't be so bad, except they all strut around town like their shit don't stink. Believe me, I know it does: when I was a kid, I worked for Jakey Marble cleaning outhouses.

"This town used to be a good place, full of honest, hardworking people. But those fuckers from Taxachusetts and Connecticunt and Screw York — those dollar-humping, flatlander bastards — began moving up here. Before you know it, everything went to hell. They bought up most the good land and started building shit like that damned barrel factory you work at.

"I've thought of getting the hell out. Thought hard. But I'm too old for that kind of shit. I need to stay put. Just wish to hell that it was like it was twenty, thirty years ago. I suppose that people like Freddy Mallory have been part of the problem."

I nodded, eking out a barely whispered "yut," and Leon went on. "I didn't have no use for Freddy Mallory. You know that. But he done a little good around here. It ain't exactly a shame, but the man didn't need to die before his time.

"When you've been in this job long as I have, you learn to keep an eye on the boys in town as they grow up. I been watching you, Earl. I know you've had it rough. I knew Bub, knew what a mean bastard he was. Beyond being a sonuvabitch, he wasn't much. Frank ain't much either; not these days, anyways. Matter of fact, Earl, when you've been in this job long as I have, you find that most people ain't much.

"But you, you're somethin', Earl. You been carrying yourself like a man since you were twelve years old. I know it, and I admire it. But I ain't got no use for that friend of yours. Denny Gamble is a piss-poor excuse for a man, and it pains me to see you get mixed up in shit like this. I know you didn't do nothin', and I know you didn't see nothin' — Katie Mallory told me that much — but you and him are thicker'n mosquitoes out to Cedar Swamp. When Walt told you and Kate that Mallory'd been killed, you knew who did it, same way we know he did it. Why else did you run off this morning? For your sake, Earl, I hope you didn't find him. I hope you ain't hiding Denny Gamble."

I stared at Leon, my ears and face flushed, his words giving off heat. It was a powerful thing to hear the truth about Denny — even if it was only half the truth — spoken out loud.

"Know the first time I got a bad feeling about him?" Leon said. "That day I caught the two of you shooting that BB gun at Moses over to Robie's Road. Crazy old bastard's got enough problems — standing up there on that boulder for ten hours at a whack, preaching from the Old Testament — and there's Denny Gamble pumping BBs at him, both of you laughing like jackasses. You sounded like a fool kid, but Denny Gamble sounded like a wild animal.

"I can handle the Frank Sargents and Freddy Mallorys of this world, Earl. But Denny Gamble. If I thought for a second that that friend of yours was gonna lay into me, I'd kill him on the spot. And the world'd be a better place for it."

◢ 16

FRANK LAY in the dark, staring at the ceiling as he waited on the B & M. At least that — the northbound freight — hadn't been taken from him.

Oh, there was plenty he longed for: watching the wasps tend the eaves; waking up to rustling in the kitchen and the smell of bacon and eggs frying; listening to the ballgames out to the porch with Earl; the shack itself. The shack. That's what he'd always called it even after it'd gotten bigger — out of hand, really — than lots of houses in town. But a thing is what it is, and the shack was a shack.

Frank had built that shack. And it looked it: a loving madman's quilt.

First there was the square box of the living room, the original tarpaper shack. The other half of the downstairs, the kitchen and such, had been added later and looked to be straining to fall off, a mutt on a choke chain. Frank had also nailed the front door shut.

"Real New Hampshire folks use the back door," Frank said. "I don't want no truck with anyone who's banging on my front door."

The upstairs, by itself, looked okay — square, even. But

where the downstairs sagged to the right, the upstairs sagged to the left.

"Well," Frank said, "there are shacks, and then there are shacks."

When he was drinking and could get a couple of buddies to listen, the shack was all Frank would talk about. "Built all this with my own two hands," he'd say, holding up his hands as if they were proof. "Can you believe it? My own two hands." Never mind that the shack looked as if it had been built from a blueprint flapping on a clothesline.

In some ways, it wasn't so much the shack he missed as the idea of the shack. For a man like Frank, who'd spent so many years on the road, it was magic to live in the belly of a place that he'd built himself. Earl would sometimes catch him standing in the dooryard, all nods and smiles, proud-eyeing the place.

Often, though, especially as his gut and arms began to sag and give in to the years, it seemed to Frank that it couldn't have possibly been him who'd driven every nail, planed every board, and laid every shingle. The shack had grown so, how could it have been him? Maybe it had grown on its own somehow, drawing what it needed from the earth. Frank wouldn't discount that story; it was as good as any other.

When he had felt that way, overwhelmed by what he'd built because he no longer believed that he'd truly built it, he would shut all the lights and walk from room to room, like a blind man, touching: the walls, the windowsills, the door casings. His horny hands grazing the wood and remembering: the grain, the knots, and the sawdust — like the fine powder that dusted the wings of the moths and millers that clung to the screen door summer nights. In missing the shack, there in the County Farm, what Frank most longed for was to touch that wood which for so many years he'd bent to his needs. In that longing, Frank thought of his father:

Frank and his dad are at a lumberyard, and Frank's old man pulls out a board, rubs it, and says, "Now ain't that a nice piece of lumber, Frankie? Just touch that. Ain't that nice?" Frank's embarrassed for his father, doesn't understand why he's so excited about feeling up a piece of wood.

Frank laughed there in the dark, chewing on his shame. He'd forgotten that day, and most like them, the same way he'd forgotten whether he'd built his shack. Each night, as he waited for the B & M, only a half mile into those woods beyond his window, he walked through his past the same as he'd walked through the shack. Instead of getting drunk on whiskey or beer every night, Frank Sargent got drunk on the past, which packs a wallop for a man who hasn't spent much time there. Frank would get so wound up with the thinking that he needed that last train through — singing its hymns to some unknown future — to lull him to sleep.

He closed his eyes, waiting, and he's fifteen again, living with his grandfather, his ma's old man, in Gorham. Down to the well fetching water, he grunts as he hefts the cement plug from the top of the well. A skinny piece of clothesline is tied to the handle of the five-gallon bucket he lowers into it. The pail bobs and sways once it hits the water, but he jiggles the rope, and the pail lists and begins to fill, finally sinking. Tying the rope around a belt loop on his dungarees, he sits on the edge of the well and stretches his legs. He plucks a blade of grass from the ground, holds it to his lips, and blows, making kazoo noises. After a few minutes he stands up, wipes the sweat from his forehead with a swipe of his arm, and pulls up the full bucket, drawing the rope through his right hand and pulling with his left, then drawing through the left and pulling with the right. He feels his arm muscles work — swelling and relaxing, swelling and relaxing. He looks into the well, remembers someone told him once that if you go down a well during the day, you can see the stars. He figures it's bullshit. But he wouldn't mind seeing the stars during the day if it's true. When the pail's up, he unties the rope, coils it, and loops it round his left shoulder. He bends down and scoops the cold, clear water into his mouth. When he's done drinking, he splashes the water on his face and neck, grabs the pail, and lugs it up the rutted path to the house.

When Frank reaches the top of the hill, his grandfather is sitting on the front steps and it's as if Frank is seeing him for the first time: a thin mat of curly, white hair clings to a chest that's turned into droopy, old man tits; his arms have lost their tone; and his gut has turned into rolling hills of fat — a body that's seen better days, a body that's been used. Frank looks at his own arm muscles, puffed out like pride with work, and wonders what his grandfather is thinking as he looks at him.

Frank always seemed to sense the train a split second before he could hear it, the way he knew it was about to rain before he'd even felt a drop. He didn't know whether the train made some slight tremor in the air or if his mind played tricks.

The B & M's warning whistle wailed — harsh, sharp. Soon, though, it softened into the pining of sad but kindly ghosts who sounded like they were aching for their unrecoverable pasts, spent like shotgun shells. True, the B & M spoke to Frank of wasted years. But, too, the train was headed north. To Frank, north was the direction of the future. As he tried to sort those B & M-induced notions, Frank dropped off to sleep, long before the train faded north into the night, into the future.

◢ 17

ME AND DENNY were at least half an hour deep into the swamp, the night air heavy as a full udder. We weren't running, really, but we hustled along, like we'd broke out the County Farm and the hounds had been sicked on our tails. Denny dogged me, his breath coming harsh and hard. But he didn't bitch — Denny had always been game — and we pushed deeper.

In daylight, if you work at it, you can almost get to know the swamp. Its mystery will surrender to the familiar. During the day . . .

But come dusk, you have to give in to the swamp, the uncertainty of night. The trails — by day as easy to follow as the gullied path that runs down to the well from the shack — squirm like snakes impaled on a pitchfork, the trees bend closer, the puckerbrush rustles, your breathing stills. The dark shuts behind you — spilled ink — and it looks like you'll never get back home. But soon the night vision comes, eyes greedily sucking in the light to feed that hunger to see, and the swamp becomes a shadow land. The mystery deepens, weasels its way into your gut, and dredges up the varnish-and-wood smell of pews, the leather-and-pulp reek of Bibles and hymnals; and I see the pastor's fleshy, baby-belly-smooth paw swallow my small hand, see the blood blossom on the crude-carved Jesus nailed to the church's back wall. But that moment passes, because the mystery runs deeper than their Bible learning and their shacks of God — no holier than Frank Sargent's tarpaper abortion. What's left is that uncertainty of night, the snake-backed paths.

Denny had showed some hours after Leon drove off. Strange how things work out. I guess I'd expected a fierce argument, a fistfight. But anger withers, droughts end:

Asleep on the porch, I wake up and Denny's there in the dark, standing over me, a silent shadow. We look to each other, nothing to say, both of us worn down by the summer, the heat, the killing — Denny worse than me. He's been stripped to the raw, the way you'd strip paint off an old chair. I remember Frank always saying, "There's worse than being unhappy, Earl. Remember that."

Denny needs my help, I know, and I nod towards Cedar Swamp. That's where we have to go. A body can lose himself there, even Denny Gamble.

I heard the *slap, slap* of water hitting land; then I was out of the woods, Center Marsh stretching before me. I stared into the dark, sucked in the musty smell, as Denny lurched after me. When I looked at him right then, I wanted to spit in his face. I wanted the Denny Gamble from the night before, the cocky bastard who'd gutted Freddy Mallory, not the pussy leaning against a tree, coughing and wheezing. Seeing him like that made me want to hurt him.

I had a cousin made me feel that way when I was a kid.

She was stupider'n rocks, and I sure didn't like getting near her. It was like I thought I'd get as soft as she was if I got too close, might catch whatever it was made her spend three years in first grade.

Anyway, one day I'm playing with my cowboys and Indians over to Grandpa Ora's and I hear Marie tramp up the steps. I must've been five; that would've made her seven. When she gets to the top of the steps, she says in that lazy whine of hers that gives every word she says at least twice as many syllables as it's supposed to have, "Hi-iii, Er-rull." She grins like a dog eating shit.

"Hi, Marie," I says, knocking over my cowboys and Indians and stuffing them quick into two White Owl cigar boxes. One box for the cowboys, one for the Indians.

"Wan-na play-ay?" she asks.

I look at her, look at my cowboys and Indians, which I figure she's made me put away by showing up. So I stand up, stomp within smelling distance of her, and punch her in the stomach hard as I can. But she doesn't say nothing, just stands there, her eyes getting wet. I hit her two more times; tears water her cheeks. It's after that third punch, when she doesn't try to move, doesn't even flinch, that I know she'll let me keep hitting her till my arm falls off. My ears and cheeks burn with the knowing, and I start to cry, too.

There was something about Denny standing there in the swamp, hugging that tree, gasping, that brought out the miserable sonuvabitch in me, made me want to smack him in the gut a couple times the way I had Marie. But that hard-assed feeling passed once Denny walked over. Something about the way he carried himself made me feel like an asshole for even thinking about slugging him. The set of his jaw suggested that he'd decided something; it jutted out some — proud, defiant. My skin crawled, but I couldn't figure why.

Denny stripped, his sweat-drenched T-shirt shredding as he tugged it off. I looked at him, the question in the tilt of my head. He nodded. I took a deep breath, stared hard at him through the dark, and stripped too. I piled my clothes in a lump, sat on 'em. Denny sat down across from me — a ballicky bare-assed ghost — and our final mosquito game began.

The first mosquito brushed my skin as light as the first time I kissed a girl's nipple. The second one settled on my right arm north of the wrist. I closed my eyes as she sawed through my skin, jammed feeding tubes into my vein, sucked. I imagined her, flush with my blood, withdrawing and flying drunk-wild out over Center Marsh, just shy of the water, where a bass would strike and steal away with her and my warm blood to the lake's chill womb. I shuddered. Two more lit on my arm, gentle as the first. At least a couple, in full mosquito whine, danced at my ears. They plunged their needle-noses into my face, my legs, my ass, between my toes — everywhere. They swiped my blood, gorged themselves. I doubled my fists and gritted my teeth as swells of sweat broke over my face. But I sat still, goddammit, back straight, mouth shut, as they bit and buzzed, sucked and soared, billowing from the swamp. I wondered how many mosquitoes clung to me, rubbing their front legs together the way a Boy Scout will rub sticks, feasting, blushing from brown to red. They creeped, crawled — on my face, in my hair, ears, nose — leaving only itchy medals. I dug my hands into the damp earth — even in the drought the swamp held its water — squeezed it, let it ooze between my fingers. I tightened my jaw as the mosquitoes kept coming, thrusting their small swords into me. I was like one of those guys over to the Deerfield Fair who climbs into a wicker basket, then some broad with big tits Jell-O-ing out of her bikini bangs swords into the basket as the crowd stares, paying more attention to her straining hogans than to the swords — which is the trick to it, I suppose.

I opened my eyes. Denny sat as still as I did. I'd half expected to see him rocking back and forth, hugging himself like he'd just hauled ass out of Granite Lake in April before it had shed all its ice. But he wasn't; this wasn't the Denny Gamble of the arms-folded smirk. His face gave away nothing through its mosquito mask, but he still put me on edge. There was a thing unsaid — unasked — between us. But Denny, as unknowable as the swamp, sat there rigid, seeming to accept that his madman summer had brought him to this mosquito game.

I looked away, above the swamp, and saw clouds bully their way across the sky that extinguished the stars one by one, then the moon, making the swamp as black as the pit under the blaster. The mosquitoes swarmed.

The itch was deep. Not the easy itch of a scab or poison ivy — Grandpa Ora'd called it poison ivory — not the kind of itch that'd give in to Mercurochrome or calamine lotion. It gnawed at the bone, smoldered under the surface like a dump fire. An itch that'd have to be rooted out, stamped on. An itch that made a body think about dying. Some dizzy, like I might puke, I closed my eyes, fell into that sweaty, fitful twilight between wakefulness and true sleep:

It's late one summer night when Denny and me are still kids. We've tied Budweiser cans to the soles of our high-top sneakers. We scuff along Main Street through the sleepy Plains, our feet spitting sparks as we scrape the cans on the blacktop. Seems we tramp about town all night long, friends walking towards morning, wobbling on what we fancy is our own private lightning.

*

I started awake and saw that what'd been unsaid between me and Denny had taken shape.

Denny held my old man's knife. Not threatening, mind you, just holding it. Right palm flat, facing the sky — a hand feeling for rain — and the haft resting there as if he were weighing the knife, deciding something. Was it stained with Mallory's blood, I wondered. Or had Denny cleaned it?

Nothing fancy, that knife. Ugly, strong, built for hard work. The broad, flat blade — tobacco-juice brown, stained, pitted — looked like it'd been ripped from the jaws of some great old man-eating beast; the haft was grainy oak gone dull. My old man had shined that handle till you could see shadows square-dance on it. It was the knife that Bub had carved on me with; the knife Ma'd chased me with when she'd had her breakdown; the knife Frank had turned on Ma that last time. My family's history, a bloody scrapbook, that knife didn't rest easy in no outsider's hand. Denny had no rights to it.

First time I saw that knife I was no more than six years old:

After dark, late October, brittle leaves — pushed by the wind — crab-walk across the dooryard; trees low; and the full moon, headlight-white except for its birthmark, seems to block out the eastern sky. Bub takes me to the barn and we stand at his workbench, which has the same cigarette and sawdust smell as him. The barn's dark, but we're splashed by moonlight that swarms through the one window.

Bub says, "Ma says you been sassing her."

I know better than to say anything.

"I don't like no smart-mouth, Earl," he says. "You ought to know that by now."

My ears get warm, my muscles tighten — getting ready for the beating I know is coming.

"Sounds to me, son, like you got yourself an alligator mouth and a hummingbird ass." He pauses. "Pull down your pants."

I reach to unbuckle my belt, balk.

"I said pull those pants down, goddammit, or I'll do it for you. Underwear, too."

Goose pimples sprout on my legs and butt; my balls shrivel, burrow into my crotch. I don't see where it comes from, but the knife is in his hand, the moonlight making that blade look like a sliver of sun-spattered brook, the kind of fast water that's so cold it hurts your teeth to drink it. I look at the knife, at my pruny balls, the knife again. I remember the pigs I saw them de-nutting over to Vernon Collins's the year before: four men wrestling down the pig, and my old man moving in with the knife. I start to cry.

"Turn around," Bub says.

The blade is cold on my ass and I jump. I hear my blood drip slow onto the barn floor.

That was the first time. Wasn't the last. Oh, Bub wasn't soft, didn't do it too much. He never cut me stitches deep. Bit me just enough to make me scared, to make me glad when he used his fists instead of carving on my back, my butt, my belly. By the time he run out on us, that knife had made me look like I'd spent most of my life fucking barbed wire. Me and that knife, we were intimate. And there it lay in Denny's right hand.

A wind kicked up, keeping the mosquitoes at bay. It keened high above Center Marsh. Clouds boiled in the sky. I looked in Denny's eyes — the wind gusted harder, the clouds rolled, turned in on themselves — and that's when I think I knew what he wanted, even though I didn't know I knew, because I shivered and the gooseflesh stippled my body the way it had that first time with Bub and the knife. I wanted to have the guts to stand up, go over, take the knife, and hug goddamned sonuvabitching Denny Gamble. But his fisher-cat eyes said stay away until I ask for you, said the knife still has a taste for Earl Duston, still has hard work to do.

The wind stopped of a sudden. Just like that. One second gusting like a little kid gabbing a mile a minute, and the next it stopped in midblow, that same little kid smacked upside the head by his old man and told to shut up.

Me and Denny sat hunched in the center of the quiet, maybe the only living things in the swamp right then. Alone in her black heart. This wasn't just a couple of kids screwing around at the edge of Cedar Swamp, playing a cheap version of the mosquito game. We were part of the mystery. I was afraid.

Denny gripped the knife, waggled it up and down like he was testing its balance. I watched him the way I would a mosquito stealing my blood. He pirouetted the tip of the blade on that softness just below his navel, drawing blood, marking the spot.

He offered me the knife, handle first, his request on the table.

I flushed with the knowing. My mouth went to cotton, my head took to pounding, and my hands turned sweat-slick. There was everything to be said and nothing. I looked to his face, saw how much he hurt. I'd always known that. Guess that's why I never gave up on him, even with all the bullshit. You can't turn your back on a friend who's hurting.

"Earl."

The voice was that of a body who's been scraped raw and acid's been rubbed into his wounds. I couldn't refuse him.

I took the knife and cut.

◢ 18

I BURIED DENNY in the swamp. I hacked hanks of black, damp swamp soil from the earth till there was room for the swamp to take him; it wasn't no six foot deep, but it weren't shallow neither. Buried the knife with him. And once I had him safe and secure in the swamp's womb, just after I'd tamped his grave with my bare feet, the black earth pushing up between my toes, it began to rain.

I sat there in the swamp in the downpour, the rain's cool fingers tapping my back. Still night, but a gray mist hung over the woods as the rain surged down, beating steady on the water, spattering me with mud churned up as it hit the ground. I didn't mind the wet. The rain felt good on my bites, kept the mosquitoes away; I couldn't have faced them again. I listened to the rain, the constant hiss on the leaves whispering that the drought was over. It'd been one dry season, ripe with days feeling full of dust inside, days of fire searing my gut. I needed the rain as much as the land did. Off across Center Marsh, I heard the B & M. Its whistle wailed small, muted — like in a dream.

August 1975

Epilogue

I WOKE UP on the porch, the radio static-ing, the Red Sox game long over. Raining again. Steady, dependable rain — Leon George rain. I listened to it stitch the roof. It was a sound I never got tired of. Ranked right up there with frogs peeping, the B & M wailing, and cards being shuffled. Denny had made cards sing when he had a deck in his hands. I yawned, scratched my arms. Yawned again and closed my eyes, the beat of the rain putting me back to sleep.

The morning broke cool and bright after the rain. Water dripped from too-green leaves, hissed as cars splashed by, wriggled in pencil-thin streams beside the road, to finally dribble through culverts and collect in hidden pools. Sun and water had struck a balance for a change, the water feeding the still-dry land as the sun warmed it — but not too much.

But even on a day like that, the factory squatted ugly in the sandpit, an ornery lump of gray brick. A brute of a building that sucked in sunlight and spewed out crippled snakes of steam and smoke, a building that seemed to swallow the crisp breeze and smother it. The longer I worked there, the more I came to think it was alive. Some huge farting-belching monster itching to devour Granite, biding time to spread its black stain. And every day me and the other guys willingly walked into that monster's gloomy gut, fed it our sweat and muscle. I guess you could say we were pretty soft in the head.

Stain humped by in his Road Runner, blowing the horn — a-ROO-gah! — misting me with road water. I waved as best I could; my hands were still a scabby black and blue from punching out Ma's clothesline, and it pained me like the arthritis to bend my wrists. The Road Runner was a real beauty: royal blue, jacked-up ass-end, wide ovals, and mags. Stain had connived it out of Dickie — he'd bought it from Rusty after his Buick croaked — who'd quit the factory and gone down Florida to do dry wall with his uncle. Dickie had never told us he was taking off; just up and left one day. He'd needed the cash, so he sold Stain the '69 Runner cheap.

Vernon had made Stain garage foreman after old Dean got banged up pretty good when a tire jack gave way on him. And Vernon let Stain run the parts business, too. Leastways, that's what I heard. Hardly saw Stain no more — not the way I used to, anyways. He either worked his ass off over to the garage or planted himself at home to keep an eye peeled on his pining and pregnant wife. Folks said Pam had retreated to her bedroom permanent when she'd heard about Denny killing Freddy Mallory and then running off. They said she kept the shades and curtains drawn all day long, ruined her eyes by taking in the g.d. soaps, and woofed down half gallons of Hood's vanilla ice cream; I figured Stain to already be shopping around for another wife, something nice to sit with him in the Road Runner.

Man, who would've thought before the summer: Dickie

in Florida, Stain married, and Denny . . . gone. Dog? He'd been missing more and more work, sometimes sleeping a week at a whack; Johnson still wouldn't can him, though.

Looking at the factory and thinking about Dog made me feel bad, but I felt a lot worse when I saw Andy pull into the parking lot in his rust-speckled Ford Fairlane.

Andy.

We still talked about how he'd decked Johnson and walked out the door, doing what we all wanted to do but didn't have the balls. It was the first story we told new guys, how Andy rose up and struck Johnson down. It was legend, history passed worker to worker. Same as when Hank and Ed Rollins got pissed at Double Murphy and closed him in a drum. Or the time Marcel came to work lugging a bucket of garter snakes, then set them loose in the toilets. Andy's punch that floored Johnson was a shot that'd given us hope and made us feel good — at least for a while.

But Andy was back; the legend would shrivel, wither — die.

Wearing his usual work clothes, dungarees and a white T-shirt, Andy sat in his car and stared at the factory. I walked up, and he rolled down his window.

"Fuck you doing, Andy?"

He wouldn't look at me; only stared harder at the factory. He gripped the steering wheel so his knuckles turned white.

"I'm coming back," he said in a raw whisper. "I'm coming the fuck back."

"But what about Johnson?" I said.

Andy looked up, a tight smile on his face. "I don't think he'll bother me much. Do you?"

"Guess not," I said. "Christ, we still talk about what you did to him. Guys are going to be in shock."

Andy shook his head slow, a mourning shake. "I'm the

one in fucking shock," he said. "Never thought I'd come back to this pit. Never."

I winced, he hurt so bad.

"But I couldn't find a job, Earl. Couldn't find one damned job. Not much out there for a guy with a sixth-grade education. Nothing that pays decent, anyways. I got a family to support. Weren't for them, you can bet your ass I wouldn't've ever come back to this hole.

"But you don't know what it's like nowadays trying to find work. Every day it's doors slammed in your face, your old lady getting on your ass to find something, anything. Did some odd jobs, but there was nothing steady. It sucked, Earl. Totally sucked. We got behind on our bills, got the electric shut off so we couldn't even watch goddamned TV. Couldn't go nowheres, couldn't buy the kids nothing. It's getting pretty bad when you can't even afford to buy your kid a fucking comic book.

"Finally, I had to do it. Had to come back. I'm proud, but I ain't proud enough to let my kids go to bed with no supper. I broke down and called Old Man Fecteau Saturday from Joanne's sister's place. He knows I'm a worker, that I bust ass. He knows what I'm worth. And he said he'd take me back — long as I run the blaster. Said they couldn't find no one to run it good as I did.

"But I ate shit, Earl. I don't feel like a man no more. Fecteau knew I was hard up, knew he had me by the balls. And the bastard squeezed some. It was practically like begging. What kind of country is this if you have to beg for a job? I tell you, I wouldn't've done it if it weren't for Joanne and the kids."

I knew they wouldn't come, but I could hear the tears in his voice the way you can smell the rain before it pours.

"You know," Andy said. "This place'll fucking kill ya,

breathing in that shit all day long. Take your body and screw it all up. Ain't no doubt. But there's worse than working here, Earl. A man with no job, he ain't nothing. He's shit. He's dirt. The Gonyers won't even talk to a man who ain't got a job. I tell ya, there was days where . . . where I . . ."

The buzzer blatted. But Andy still didn't move.

"Just do me one favor, Earl. Quit this place for me. Tell Johnson and Old Man Fecteau and everyone else to stick it up their ass. Just fucking quit it — before it kills ya."

◢

It was that shadow time between the end of dusk and the start of night. Inky blotches asserted themselves among the dusky grays — the western sky still tainted by the dying sun. Frank stood out back the County Farm smoking. One of the guards, a Graniter who'd known Frank going on twenty years, had for some weeks been letting him stay out till lockup. Frank appreciated it. A man needs the illusion of freedom. Frank had always been a dusk man, prey to the smell of dampness and fresh-cut grass, the sound of peepers setting the night air to shimmying with frog song. Shadows suited him; he had liked nothing better than to sit on his porch and watch himself disappear as dusk deepened to night.

Frank pulled on his cigarette, conjured up another summer dusk:

The boys — there must be six, seven of them — dart and swoop in the dooryard, chase each other for no better reason than to chase each other. Because to run and sweat is better than to sit still and sweat. Dusk becomes the *slap, slap* of their sneakered feet, their giggly laughter, the panting of the chase. Someone swears — "You stupid cocksucker, Eddie!" — and they all laugh. Swear words are powerful, they know, but they're not sure why. The swearing doesn't come natural yet. Each curse is rehearsed, mulled, till you're flush and tingly with the word. Finally it comes rushing out all crude and gangly. The safest response, for both the swearer and the cursed, is to laugh, because your ears are burning and your legs have gone to rubber and you don't know why.

Frank pounces on Gary Haywood, wrestles him down, and washes his face in the dirt. The grit sticks to Gary's sweaty cheeks. There's no meanness to what Frank's doing. It's part of the game, what boys do to each other. But Gary starts to cry; he shrieks, "Get off me! Leave me alone!"

Frank jumps up like he's tackled a burlap sack of shit. The other boys stop running and shut up. Gary keeps crying, won't look up at them, his back rigid with sobs. The boys turn away, a couple start to run but stop quick as they started. Backs to Gary Haywood, they mill in the dooryard, whispering — young moths seeking light.

Finally, someone says, "Wanna see my firecrackers?"

Cow Southland says, "Bet I can hold one of those firecrackers longer'n anybody 'fore it blows up."

Cow, whose real name is Billy, is always saying shit like that, then chickening out. That's why they call him Cow — short for Coward.

Cow goes first. Frank lights the firecracker, flourishing the match before touching off the fuse. Cow throws the firecracker away before the boys can even count to one; the cracker never goes off, and the boys chant, "Dud! Dud! Dud!" That's how Cow Southland became Dud Southland.

"Screw you guys," Dud says. "Least I still got all my fingers."

The other boys make it to counts of two or three before

winging the firecrackers away. Frank is last. The boys yell, "One! Two! Three! Four!" And Frank flings it just as it explodes. He smells the gunpowder and burned paper; his ears ring and his eyes water.

"Frank's the winner!" Dud shouts. "Ain't no friggin' doubt about it. Frank's the winner."

But Gary Haywood shoves his way to the center of the circle. "My turn," he says. "What about me? It's my turn."

The boys look at each other, shrug, and give him a firecracker. Frank won't light it, but Dud does. The boys count — all except Frank, who stares at Gary's hand wrapped tight around the hissing firecracker — "One! Two! Three! Four!"

When the firecracker blows up in Gary's hand, he doesn't just cry; he wails — long, hard, and lonesome. An end-of-the-world wail that bridges the years from that summer night and becomes the cry of the B & M out behind the County Farm.

Frank's longing for the North Country stirred in him; it was worse than craving a drink. He listened for the train, closing his eyes and cocking his head to one side. The train's next moan was closer, and Frank glanced backwards. What little money he had, some fifty dollars, was sewn inside his pants leg. He felt for it. Still there.

The whistle keened, an old lover whispering new promises. He looked back at the County Farm once more. The train called again, a locomotive lullaby long and sweet that rose above the darkening woods. Frank's chest ached. He could feel the tears brewing behind his eyes. Trying to clear his head, he sucked in the dusky air.

The train's lament overwhelmed him the way a woman's giving in did. In that instant — when a woman's clothes are shed for the first time and the soft and smooth is offered —

Frank always wanted to cry, knew the first touch would make him shiver.

The train called one more time, and Frank ran. He thrashed through the sticky August corn and into the nightening woods, running down the path towards the train tracks, his head pounding with that angry, Frank-Sargent-surviving-another-day blood.

Home, he thought. I'm going home.

He saw himself working the woods again, rising with the sun, sleeping at sundown. And the meals: steak and venison, corn on the cob slathered with butter, fried potatoes, homemade bread, all the beer you could drink . . . No! He'd stay off the bottle this time. This time'd be different. The woods, flexing your muscles, swinging the ax, guiding the saw. That's what he wanted, that life back.

So he ran: head down, work boots thudding, legs almost buckling, arms windmilling, chest smoldering. And, wheezing and heaving, he made the cliffs above the railroad.

The train whistle howled, vibrating in his gut and making his head swim the way a good bottle of whiskey did, as the B & M rumbled by down below. He didn't have time to scramble down the path. He'd have to jump from up here. What was it? Fifteen foot? No problem.

Frank saw the open car stacked with hay bales coming and he crouched. He didn't even think about it.

And as he jumped, he knew he was going home. In the moment that he hung suspended in midair, he smelled those sweet big woods, heard the *chunk, chunk* of ax biting tree.

He grinned and knew he was free.

◢

I'd cut the headlights a mile before, but I still looked up and down Route 49 before I pulled Stain's Chevy pickup around back of Mallory's Fruit & Real Estate.

Since that night in the swamp I couldn't but breathe in Granite without unsettling Denny's ghost. And sitting there in the truck behind Mallory's, all I could see was Denny Gamble pumping hell out of Freddy Mallory's watermelons. I almost smiled.

I stepped out of the pickup, my feet crunching crushed rock. The gravestone I wanted — blacker than Denny's eyes — leaned against a link fence. I fingertipped the stone's night-cool surface and wondered how a rough hank of granite ripped from the earth's guts could be made into a thing so smooth, so perfect.

I pulled it away from the fence, felt it tug backwards. Both arms wrapped around it — practically slow-dancing with it — I tried to balance the stone upright as first it pressed against me, then lurched away.

Kate, who was helping her mother run the business, probably would have given me a deal on the stone — if I'd asked — maybe even given it to me. But you should only ask so much of a body, even one who says she loves you.

How easy those words fly out of a girl's mouth — at least once an hour it seems. In two years I'd maybe said it once to Mary Tucker — and I was drunk at the time — compared to her thousands. Mary had known how I felt about her, and I knew she felt the same. That was enough, I figured. And now Kate:

The two of us are sitting in the dampening grass under the Marrying Tree; the air smells deep green, like sex. It's late, the Durochers' house dark.

"I love it out here," Kate says. "Seems this tree could protect a body from all the world's harm."

"It's really something," I say.

"Look up into that tree this time of night, Earl, and it

seems you could shinny all the way up to heaven."

I nod, wiggle closer to her.

Kate says, "Nanna, my mother's mother, used to tell a story about a Merville Hutchins who got married out here, but then his wife took off on him. Nanna said that Merville got so nerved up about it that he tried to cut down the Marrying Tree, but the tree blunted his chain saw. Then he tried to burn it down, but the fire wouldn't take, even though he'd soaked the bark with gasoline. And when he tried to chop it down, his ax heads — not the handles — splintered. Finally, Nanna said, one night he scrambled up the Marrying Tree, vanished into those dark leaves and branches, and was never seen again. What do you suppose that story means, Earl?"

I say, "Can probably mean whatever you want it to mean. That's the way with stories. Folks take the truth of a story like that, then try to wedge it onto their own truth."

"But what do *you* think it means?" Kate asks.

I close my eyes and think for some seconds. "It's about running away," I say. "It's about giving in, running off."

"You ever want to run, Earl?"

"No."

"What if I'm pregnant?"

"No, I said."

"But what if I am?"

"I'm never going to run, goddammit! I make my own way in this world! I don't run!"

"Earl, it's okay. I believe you. Calm down."

"I seen too much running. I'm sick of the fucking running."

Kate hugs me hard, whispers humid in my ear, "I love you, Earl Duston."

We make love under the Marrying Tree — fierce granite

love, two rocks smacking together and giving off sparks. When we're done, Kate holds me in for as long as she can, like she never wants me to leave.

Anyways, Kate or no, I wanted to steal that gravestone. Denny Gamble, of all people, deserved a stolen stone to mark his grave.

I backed the truck close as I could, then tipped the stone so it leaned against the dropped tailgate. I meant to get a little leverage and slide the stone up into the pickup's bed. No sweat.

Skooching low — knees bent, butt brushing the fence — I worked my hands under the gravestone, got a grip, and lifted regular — strong, but no straining. The stone didn't budge.

I stood up, stretched, shook my shoulders a couple times, and got back down. Before I took my grip again I picked up a couple handfuls of crushed rock, rolled them around; made my hands less slippery. I muckled ahold of it again (weight forward on my toes), took one deep breath (jiggling my arm muscles), took another deep breath (gritting my teeth), and I jumped on that third breath with a grunt and lifted hard as I could: arms, back, and stomach drawn tight, sneakers burrowing into the ground, chest and right cheek flush to the cool granite, neck cords banjo-string rigid.

It moved some, and I grunted again, shifting my feet to get a better angle. She wouldn't go. But I kept at it till I got that pain in the center of my crotch that seems you're going to bust in two. That's when I give up and let her drop.

Out of breath, hands on knees, I knew I'd given it my best shot. I wasn't taking that bastard nowheres by myself. And if I couldn't do it alone, it wasn't worth doing.

"Need some help?"

I must have jumped a good three foot in the air, and my bladder loosened considerable; my heart had leaped out my mouth and hoofed it off somewheres towards Lamprey.

"What the fu . . . ?"

"It's just me, Earl," Leon George said. "Only me."

I looked up and saw Leon, arms folded, slouched against one of the sheds out back of Mallory's.

"Leon . . . I . . ." I said.

"Don't tell me nothing," he said, holding up his hand like a traffic cop. "Old hunter like me knows how to read the trail. Don't go drawing me no pictures."

"Christ, Leon . . ."

"I come here laying for Denny Gamble," Leon said, but he trailed off, too.

The two of us stood there quiet in the dark. A necessary quiet, one of preservation. But I was used to those deep silences, as black and treacherous as those water-filled quarries that lay, half forgotten, in the Granite woods. I grew up on those silences, sought safety in them.

Leon pawed at the ground, shifted his weight. Finally, he said, "That gravestone for him?"

I nodded.

We didn't say a word as we hefted the stone into the pickup.

◢

Azalea Kelley squats in her rowboat. She lifts her head slow, looks me in the eye. She seems as old as the swamp, as time itself.

"Come with me," she rasps.

She pulls us strong and even over the Center Marsh calm. We beach at Mahone's Landing and tramp a rugged two miles into the puckerbrush, which opens out onto the purest stretch of swamp I've ever seen:

This is the old swamp, the true swamp — the beginning place. Mist spurls off the water, and the bleeding sun sits perfect round on top of the trees; pools of red sun ripple between the giant rotten stumps, setting the water afire. These are the biggest, oldest stumps in the swamp, jagged, some jutting a good ten foot in the air; the tree trunks — hundreds of them — look like the ragged remains of some barricade that's been breached: splintered, bent, bowed.

I suck in that sweet swamp stink of decay. But it isn't quite right — there's another smell, too, something familiar, something wrong.

Azalea wades into the water, but it doesn't splash right. Instead of sloshing, it attacks her, claws at her, sticks to her.

She lunges into the swamp up to her chin, and when she stands back up she's clutching the biggest snapping turtle I've ever seen, its razor beak resting on her shoulder and its tail brushing her knees. It seems they're wrestling, but it's only Azalea struggling to hold on to the snapper, which is dead — smeared with toxic muck.

The drum-factory smell breaks over me full: and I see bass and pickerel washed ashore; a shitpoke, its wings sludge-soaked, squawking; steel drums lurk just under the surface. The quiet before death. Cancer. My swamp has cancer.

I throw up before I start to cry.

I woke up gagging, eyes heavy with tears. The nightmare, which had the kick of one of my true dreams, churned in my gut; right there, in deep night, I couldn't deny its truth.

I got up and took a leak; maybe I could piss away the poison that leached from the nightmare. I felt some better afterwards.

I poked my head in Ma's room on the way back. She wasn't there. She hadn't been home in at least three days.

But that was okay, she hadn't been to see Frank since Leon took him away to the County Farm.

"Me and Rollie are having a good time" is what she'd told me the week before. And I hadn't seen any black eyes or bruises — yet — so I more or less believed her.

I fell back to sleep watching Crusty stalk the moonlight caught in the oak branches outside my window.

◢

At sunrise — the nightmare gnawing fresh — I stood before Cedar Swamp one last time. Denny's gravestone lay at my feet.

A mosquito lit on my arm; I smacked it, flicked it off.

I picked up one end of the stone, stood it up straight, pushed it forward, and it hit the ground with a *whoomp*. I was four feet into the swamp, four feet closer to Denny's burying place. Picked up the other end of the stone, did the same thing — another four feet.

Again: four feet more.